Katz Tales
Beginnings

Katz Tales
Beginnings

Robert A. Boyce Jr.

Cover Artist: Mayank Sharma

Robert A. Boyce Jr.
2015

First Printing: 2015

ISBN 978-0-9966676-0-9 (Lulu Paperback)

ISBN 978-0-9966676-1-6 (Amazon Paperback)

Ordering Information:
Special discounts are available on quantity purchases by corporations, associations, educators, and others. For details, contact the publisher at the above listed address.

U.S. trade bookstores and wholesalers: Please contact Robert Boyce email: robert.boyce17@gmail.com.

Contents

Arc I: UNIFIED FRONTS
Chapter 1: Another Assault.............................3

Chapter 2: The Boss 11

Chapter 3: Military Attack 17

Chapter 4: Turning Tides.............................25

Chapter 5: Siege.............................30

Chapter 6: Fall of the Titans.............................39

Arc II: ENTER THE DRAGON
Chapter 7: Revisit 53

Chapter 8: Origins 62

Chapter 9: The Towers.............................71

Chapter 10: Dark Designs 77

Chapter 11: Merger of the Sea Beast............................84

Chapter 12: Freedom 91

Arc III: BEGINNINGS
Chapter 13: Homecoming 101

Chapter 14: Strike Three............................ 109

Chapter 15: Darkness Rises 117

Chapter 16: Transformation 128

Chapter 17: An Unlikely Union 135

Chapter 18: Resurrection 143

Chapter 19: Beginnings 150

Arc I: UNIFIED FRONTS
Chapter 1: Another Assault

The steady beat of rain pelts the ground while the roars and screams of a stampede of people surge through the Chicago city streets. Amongst torn apart cars and small smoldering fires two men stand across at a city square. As the smoke is blown to the side the large hulking man covered in red skin reaches down grabbing a car he lifts it in one hand, his muscles rippling down his arm.

"Brutilus stop!!" Yells the voice from across the square, as a man covered in bruises and ripped gold and green clothing looks over holding his hand out.

Brutilus smirks, "You got in my way Landlord…now die!" The car spirals across the square, slamming into a building as Landlord leaps over it with ease soaring into the sky.

Brutilus looks back with anger on his red face as he rears back jumping into the air after his foe. Landlord sways to the side avoiding Brutilus before dashing down after him tackling him from behind Landlord rams Brutilus into the ground. Police sirens ring through the area as they encircle the square taking up positions behind their car doors. Bullets rush over the ground hitting Landlord and Brutilus with a heavy barrage of metal and gunpowder.

Each bullet falls flat while the two roll across the ground. Brutilus lands on top of Landlord holding him down with one arm he reels back tightening his muscles as he makes a heavy fist. Landlord rests his left palm on the ground sending out a small pulse. Vines rise from the grass wrapping around Brutilus's arm they pull him back allowing Landlord to slip out from underneath. Landlord quickly rises to his feet charging in he strikes Brutilus with a running knee to the chest. The blow impacts with tremendous force pushing Brutilus back while Landlord spirals out of control and into a wall.

"This isn't going to be easy, "Landlord says while pulling himself from the wall a trickle of blood drops down from his lower lip as the rubble falls from around his body.

He dusts off his black hair while looking up to see Brutilus floating through the air coming towards him. Landlord encases himself in a dome of dirt and rock as Brutilus lands with a heavy thud smashing his fist into the wall. The earth dome begins to crack open revealing Land-lord in the corner.

Brutilus smirks driving his fist forward with tremendous force. The punch sails in towards Landlord only to hit a wall of psychic energy. The wall sends a shockwave back towards Brutilus knocking him over and sending him rolling across the road and into the building across the street. Landlord gets up looking around he sees his friend descending from above. His blue cape twirls through the air as he lands next to Landlord.

His blue and light grey outfit shimmers in the darkness of the day while his orange and red hair falls around his forehead. He glances over to Landlord while scratching his head. "Arrived just in time aye Land-lord? So what's up?"

"Brainstorm good to see ya! Brutilus is running amuck if we don't do something the military will get involved." Landlord responds with haste in his voice, "I've tried next to everything to calm him but nothing works he's on a mission today."

Brainstorm rubs his chin deep in thought he shifts his hazel eyes around scanning the area. "I sent a message to Tyreal he will be here shortly. Then we should be able to detain him. Keep him confined to one area to minimize the damage. I'll try and tap into his mind and bring him down gently. If I can't we will be on defense till Tyreal arrives to end this."

Landlord nods in approval as Brutilus rips through the wall breath-ing heavily he squints at Brainstorm. "You all know…I can hear you pretty well. Your plan won't work. If you would simply get out of my way I would continue on my straight path to Katz's hideout. A few shat-tered and ruined buildings are nothing to worry about. They will get it fixed later. I have one goal and one only. So move."

Brainstorm nods at Landlord within a second the two takeoff dash-ing along the ground Brainstorm jumps as Landlord slides across the ground spinning quickly he strikes with a swift kick towards Brutilus's chest. Brutilus grabs his leg stopping Landlord easily while Brainstorm comes down from above delivering a solid punch across Brutilus's face. Brutilus staggers slightly losing his grip on Landlord.

Free from his foe, Landlord quickly capitalizes creating a pillar of earth beneath Brutilus tossing him into the air. Brainstorm focuses his energy, turning his eyes purple; he causes the clouds above begin to swirl with energy and thunder booms across the city of Chicago. Several large lightning bolts race down striking Brutilus in the back; they force him to the ground slamming him hard against the concrete.

Brainstorm then tries to open his mind linking to Brutilus he steps into his head appearing within his mental plane. Brainstorm walks around searching through rooms of experiments and Harvard files while looking for Brutilus, a wall opens before him as he walks in. Sitting in a chair while performing an experiment is an older man he turns his chair around leaving the test tubes on the table as he stares at Brainstorm. His brown beard dips down below his chin as he pushes up his glasses sliding out of his chair he grabs his hat from the top hook next him placing it on his bald head then he folds his arms behind his long brown trench coat.

"Hmm…is there something I can help you with Brainstorm?" He says with a bored look on his face.

Brainstorm shifts his eyes around the room looking for any traps before opening his mouth, "Dr. J. Hawkins in the proverbial flesh I guess. Why are you doing this; you need to get control of Brutilus!"

Hawkins chuckles before walking over to Brainstorm he waves his plump white fingers signaling for Brainstorm to follow him. Brainstorm tags after him as the two walk down a mental corridor and into a large open room completely barren. The walls glow with a soft grey hue as they arrive at the center of the room. Hawkins stands before Brainstorm he bulks up transforming into the massive red man named Brutilus. Hawkins then takes a seat putting on his glasses he laughs.

"What you don't get dear Brainstorm is that we are one in the same. I have always had full control because it is me. I am Brutilus and Brutilus is Hawkins! I do what I want because I don't care, appealing to my emotions or my mental state will change nothing."

Hawkins speaks with elegance as he smirks and pulls on his moustache. "You know that I have a history with that man. I was the best researcher and scientist Harvard had ever seen, and he took it all from me. I had nothing left to protect myself when I worked on that project. Now look at me, this is the end result. I have become a beast, filled with spite and hatred; but unlike you I don't swear by any code. I know what I want and I will have it.

"Now that we are done here you can get out of my mind and you may refer to me as Hawkins rather than that deplorable primitive name of Brutilus I would respond much better. Thank you and have a nice day!"

Brainstorm nods, "I'll relay the name message and I'll make sure that we don't call you by that name…but really we need to stop this."

Hawkins tries to banish Brainstorm from his mind, but Brainstorm remains being firmly planted he walks over to Hawkins. "You can't get rid of me that easily. The mind is mine to manipulate my powers are nearly limitless here."

Hawkins shrugs, "You exaggerate the point is you are a fool to believe such. I wonder, while you are trapped in here what could be going on outside…? I bet you think that only a few milliseconds has passed, whether or not that is the case is something you will have to find out. Know this though, my strength and powers grow the more I desire to hurt or are annoyed by someone. I'm fueled by spite and the longer you all stand in my way the more difficult it will be for you all to survive."

Brainstorm shifts his thoughts back to the real world where he finds Landlord smashed under Hawkins's foot. He shakes his head before quickly leaving Hawkins' mind he reappears in front of the massive red skinned man. Hawkins stands taller and bigger than before.

Landlord struggles to free himself but Hawkins grabs him picking him up from the ground, he smashes Landlord into a bus. He then turns his attention towards Brainstorm but a slew of heavy metal chains slink out of a dark alleyway the chains spiral around Hawkins tying around his waist and arms they pull him to the ground.

Out of the alley steps a man shrouded in smoke. His black and red garments twirl down his body a long swirling cape drapes down to his knees as he walks forward slowly. The sound of metal clashes against the alleyway as the dark figure steps out onto the road. A mask covers his face leaving only his green eyes visible chains drag along the ground behind him. He raises his hand when suddenly a plethora of chains reach out wrapping around Hawkins they tether him to the ground. Brainstorm hurries over to Landlord helping him to his feet as the man shrouded in smoke walks over.

"That should hold him for a while. We need to remove him from the city before he causes more damage." The shrouded man says while his eyes grow sharp.

Brainstorm nods, "Good job Tyreal let's see how we can get rid of him we have to move fast before his strength increases."

As the three move in, the rain begins to fade over the area news choppers circle above watching the action and on top of a building looking down stands three men wearing long black cloaks they stare over the edge of the building watching the battle unfold. One of them removes his hood revealing his freckled face and lightly brown spiked hair. He looks over to another nodding before returning his vigil to the battle below.

The second young man removes his hood as well with jet black hair flapping in the wind a small scar sits on the left side of his face and a short moustache rests under his nose. He reaches into his pocket pulling out his glasses; he places them on his face. His wristband blinks as he raises it to his face looking over the message.

"Arcos we have to go. Titallic take your hood off and get ready. The mission is simple defeat Brainstorm and his lackeys then let Hawkins continue on. Boss has plans for him," The man says as he strips his cloak revealing his small skinny frame in a black and green suit. Two small green strips dance down his shirt along with a green lightning bolt along his right arm. His heavy black boots teeter off the side of the building as he steps along the ledge looking for an opportunity to attack.

Arcos cocks his head to the side with the roll of his eyes. "Boss better reward us for this. I'm tired of taking orders dealing with these fools. There are far more pressing concerns like what are we going to eat tonight."

Titallic removes his cloak tossing it down behind him his sharp metal body gleams as the sunlight passes through the clouds. A red and yellow vest rests on his chest moving gently in the breeze he lifts his right arm flexing his metal muscles. "Let's get to this Sentry." Titallic says as he takes a step off the ledge falling towards the earth. Sentry and Arcos stare with shock before leaping off themselves flying towards the ground.

Sentry and Arcos pass by Titallic swooping in low they glide over the ground tackling Tyreal and Brainstorm through a wall. Sentry grabs Tyreal by the cape twirling him around he tosses Tyreal through a desk and into a water cooler. Tyreal rises drenched with water he twists the metal chains dragging behind him into a sharp spear like tendril driving it forward towards Sentry. The enemy smirks lifting his left hand he snaps his fingers. Directly before him the tendril moves forward at a snail's pace. Sentry easily walks around it stepping up to Tyreal he delivers several quick jabs and a heavy kick to Tyreal's chest.

He snaps his fingers again resuming time; Tyreal is hit with each blow causing him to fall back from the combination attack. Sentry then pounces on Tyreal stomping him into the ground. Struggling to free himself, Tyreal wraps his chains around Sentry's leg forcing him to stumble as he escapes the barrage of attacks. Sentry gets up only to get hit by a strong punch from Tyreal's left fist staggering him. Tyreal sends a chain out grabbing a table he pulls it in slamming table into Sentry's side and knocking him over. The wooden table shatters under the pressure of the blow leaving small wooden bits strewn across the floor.

Tyreal picks up a sharp wooden stake from the broken table spinning around his fingers he drives it down towards Sentry's heart. The weapon stops half an inch before Sentry as it slowly descends towards him Sentry shuffles his body to the side breathing heavily he gets up. As time resumes a strong knee plows into Tyreal's face knocking the wood from his hand and sending him barreling through the ceiling.

Brainstorm gets up dusting himself off he looks over at Arcos, "What's your game this time Arcos?"

Arcos shrugs; with a wave of his finger a car revs its engine. The vehicle accelerates racing into the building it slams into Brainstorm driving him through three walls and out the other side into the street. Brainstorm gets up scratched and bleeding he calls forth a massive gale of wind whistling through the destroyed walls it cuts across the rooms slicing at Arcos. Arcos ducks down as his cloak is shredded in the gale. As he stands up his silver and grey metal suits fastens to his body. The wind strikes against his metal frame but it fails to slice through as Arcos takes off flying through the building at Brainstorm. Brainstorm dodges to the side catching Arcos with a swift kick to the back sending him to the ground. Arcos grumbles while getting up, he catches a punch from Brainstorm, but Brainstorm unleashes a charge of psychic energy through his fist blowing Arcos back.

Brainstorm calls down a bolt of lightning but Arcos blocks the bolt with a bus moving it between him and Brainstorm he scratches his head.

"Well hmm...maybe I should have come at this a different way." Arcos peeks up from behind the bus to see Brainstorm rising covered in a psychic barrier.

Arcos then strikes at the barrier with a strong punch cracking the shield and launching Brainstorm back. Brainstorm regains his balance transferring the energy from the barrier he launches a beam of psychic energy at Arcos. The beam speeds pass Arcos as he sways to the side avoiding the attack the metal around his arm spirals around enclosing his hand as small lines of energy filter into the center area. A burst of energy fires from his hand crossing the sky it hits Brainstorm in the chest launching him through a glass wall.

Titallic slams down on the ground creating a small impact crater from his weight as he pulls himself to his feet standing up he rolls his shoulders before walking forward towards Landlord and Brutilus. Titallic stands in front of Landlord checking over his weakened body he rolls his eyes.

Hawkins gets up staring directly at Titallic he quickly lifts his fist punching Landlord through a light pole and into a semi-truck. "Now that he is out of the way shall we begin?" Hawkins says with a gleam in his eyes.

Titallic crosses his arms, "I'm not here to deal with you, just him. You are to continue on your path and meet with the boss. He has many questions and what not for you."

"You think I'm here to be his patsy? Fool I'm going to ruin his life like he ruined mine!" Hawkins says with rage in his eyes.

Titallic laughs, "I doubt that you would be able to do anything to the boss, he is far more powerful than he was those couple years back; he could erase you from existence in a second."

Hawkins squints at Titallic before bursting across the ground at high speeds he throws a strong punch towards Titallic but his foe counters with a fist of his own. The two collide with such force that shockwaves ring through the streets and the ground under them cracks and breaks under the pressure. Titallic is knocked back as Hawkins barrels forward attacking again. He sways under Hawkins's large fist grabbing him with both arms he turns his back towards Hawkins pulling him over his shoulder and slamming Hawkins on the ground.

Titallic then swings his foot along the ground striking Hawkins across the stomach and pushing him into the air. Titallic leaps after Hawkins attacking with a rapid barrage of punches. Each blow lands hard against Hawkins's thick hide. Hawkins's face grows more annoyed with each blow until he smashes his elbow into Titallic's back. Titallic flies forward smashing into a flag pole his head spins around it once before dropping to the ground.

Hawkins lands behind him with a heavy thud he steps on Titallic's shiny metal chest pressing him into the ground. "Hahaha you thought you could best me? My skin is near indestructible and my strength constantly grows how did you ever hope to win!?"

Titallic rolls his eyes, "Whatever what I thinking…."

The sky above crackles with thunder as a severe bolt of electricity charges down striking both Titallic and Hawkins. The electricity runs through Titallic and back into Hawkins completely paralyzing him. Titallic flips back to his feet hitting Hawkins with a heavy kick to the chest he knocks Hawkins over.

"Ahh there we go I guess you are beaten," Titallic says with a smirk on his face.

Shortly after Arcos and Sentry fly in landing next to Titallic they take a deep breath. Sentry looks over seeing Hawkins getting up more enraged than ever. "Now would be a good time to get out of here. I saw military jets moving in from the South we will head back to the base and leave the rest to those so called heroes."

Titallic and Arcos nod in approval as the three take to the air flying off to the West.

Chapter 2: The Boss

Relief and rescue teams mount around the destroyed areas of Chicago pulling bodies from the wreckage while fire crews drown the flames around the buildings. Over at a command tent two old men sit watching the military recover efforts, one stands in green with five stars across his shoulder.

Beads of sweat drop down his forehead rolling over his left eye patch as he pounds his hand on the desk. "What the hell is this Wizencut? We need to stop this before it gets further out of control. How many people did we lose today?!"

The other man flips through a mound of papers putting his feet up on the desk, Wizencut puts on his reading glasses. His long slender fingers run across the pages scanning the information. "General Niesse you will not use such foul language with me. But to answer your question there was a reported 123 deaths from this attack. Less than the last assault if that is any consolation. Nonetheless they have eluded us again. Brainstorm and his band are helping with the recovery efforts, but does that really excuse them for helping to cause this tragedy in the first place? Anyway I have a conference with the President later, we will discuss measures to find Katz and bring them all in for execution." Wizencut gets up fixing his blue suit and putting on his admiral hat he nods at Niesse.

"I'm sorry but you know this is sickening. You know what that damn monster Katz did to my brother. He killed him, murdered in cold blood with no remorse, I was supposed to protect him and I failed. I cannot allow this to continue. We need a full intervention; I want to rip them to pieces! I'll see about scouting for their new location and maybe tracing Brutilus will yield some results." Niesse says with distain on his face. The two walk out of the tent as a helicopter descends waiting for Wizencut to jump on.

Wizencut turns towards Niesse, "I'll see if I can get aerial clearance for you in this campaign. I have already gotten the new model tanks stationed outside of the city; hopefully they will provide enough firepower to deal with this menace."

Wizencut steps onto the helicopter closing the door behind him the machine takes off sailing high into the sky and off towards the East. Far across the city of Chicago Sentry, Arcos, and Titallic fly over the pro-

jects, dusk settles over the land as they sail over a large apartment building. Behind the building lies a small desolate field with nothing more
than a small shack sitting near the curb. The three drop down in front of
the shack taking the key from under the rug Sentry opens the door. Titallic closes his eyes as the metal around his body morphs and changes
shrinking and molding itself back into flesh. He shrinks slightly appearing as a young man with black hair and smooth skin. His muscle
definition decreases as he opens his brown eyes before walking through
the door sealing the shack behind him.

The three stroll down a short corridor and down a set of stairs,
opening another door they arrive in a large room with monitors and
computers sitting against a wall. A few lights shine over the room illuminating the area, in a dark corner overlooking the computer station sits
a large recliner chair; the chair rocks back and forth slowly. A short flash
of light peeks out through the darkness from the top of the recliner as it
stops suddenly. With a loud clap the room is illuminated as the three
kneel down before the recliner a middle aged man stands up his purple
and gold cape draping down to the floor behind him as his boots shine
in the light. Golden armor sits upon his small chest with a purple undershirt covering his arms. A crown sits on top of his short afro as he
crosses his arms.

"Boss man, Hawkins is on his way…I'm not exactly sure when he
will be here, but he was last seen on the other side of the projects." Sentry says while looking up to see his brown face searching for his eyes he
notices the man is gazing up at the ceiling watching the fan spin. "Boss!
Katz! You aren't paying attention!"

Katz shakes his head coming out of a daydream he glances around
the room before waving at the three allowing them to relax. "Oh what
now…oh Hawkins yeah, well good I already have surveillance on the
area once he enters we will know. Did you all get rid of any of those
other meddlesome ingrates while you were out?"

Titallic stands up first, "Well boss, I hear they tried to kill them but
they were highly resilient to well you know dying."

Katz squints with a low grumble coming from his throat,
"hmm…well I guess that is okay. We can kill them next time. On to
more pressing things…."

"Like what we are going to eat tonight!?" Interjects Arcos as he
stands up looking down at Katz, "You know for the boss you are short-
er than all of us."

Katz squints while looking up to Arcos and Titallic. "That is not true, Sentry is the same height as me and I'm a little bit more muscular than him so there. Besides…"

Katz begins to hover looking Arcos straight in the eyes, "That doesn't mean I won't break you outright if you try me…but I probably won't anyway so let's get on with it. Joseph's tonight?"

Titallic and Sentry both look at each other with a shrug they both nod while Arcos agrees, "Sounds like a plan I haven't ate there in a month."

Katz drops back to the ground walking over to the monitors he checks the cameras as his face grows pale and his eyes grow wide. Outside Hawkins stands directly across the street from the shack, completely still he stares forward as a gust of wind blows dust and small pebbles across the ground in front of him.

Katz turns to his teammates with a timid voice and a finger up in the air, "You all should know that we are currently in a bit more danger than I thought. I was going to go out and meet him near the center of the projects but I guess he is a little bit faster than first predicted…he's across the street!!"

"What would you like us to do boss?" Sentry asks looking concerned.

Katz rolls his eyes, "There is nothing to be done, I'll just have our conversation here. You all may head out to Joseph's and I'll catch up shortly."

Sentry nods, "As you say boss."

The three get up heading towards the back exit they fly off as Hawkins jumps into the air sailing over the building he drops down smashing the shack to pieces with one blow. The roof of the underground headquarters begins to collapse as the stairwell falls in. Katz runs around sliding through the back exit as rocks collapse sealing the way out. He flies out of the ground behind the ruined shack flipping through the air he lands in front of Hawkins. The two stand apart while the wind whips Katz's cape around, Katz dusts himself off and fixes his crown before turning his full attention to Hawkins.

"Well now my old friend, what is it that brings you to my headquarters…and why did you level the building!?" Katz says with a glint of anger in his eyes, "Also how did you find me?"

Hawkins takes one step forward, "You know what you did to me Katz. Finding you was easy enough, I am a genius and your boys there aren't exactly the stealthiest people. Now why I will make you suffer, it is because of you that I am like this, because of you that my funding got cut and I was ousted! Dr. K.S. Katz boy genius that ruined my tenure at Harvard as lead researcher! You ruined the life that I built for myself, and you didn't even apologize!"

Katz rolls his eyes, "If you're going to be a child about that then I don't have any qualms about killing you now, but I would rather keep you alive you can be useful in the world to come. Hawkins, Dr. J. Hawkins, we have had a long and strenuous relationship and I can tell that it has weighed heavily on you some of the things I did… I will admit weren't at all the nicest, but you really left me with no alternative but to do what I did. You know working at Harvard and being the new scientist guy isn't exactly the easiest job in anyone's life.

"My project was just starting up, atomic energy is the future, and you were stuck on baby spite generators. What did you expect me to do, continue to let you play the piper with lives at stake? So the President cut your funding, that doesn't mean you can't continue your research, you just had to be craftier otherwise you would have been saved from that umm… little explosion was it?"

Hawkins's eyes turn red with annoyance and malice as he drives a heavy punch towards Katz. The blow strikes the ground with earthshattering force sending up a plume of dirt and earth into the darkening sky. Katz sails overhead flipping over Hawkins he lands behind him. Hawkins spins around in an attempt to smash Katz with his arm but, his foe grabs it with both arms sliding across the ground, from the force of the attack, he stops nearly falling over.

"Haha I see you have gotten better since the last time I smashed your face in." Hawkins says while twisting further back nearly knocking Katz off balance.

Katz takes off floating barely off the ground, "You think just a little better, well I'll have to show you just how far behind you are."

Katz breaks off from Hawkins landing a short distance back he charges forward. Sliding on the ground he pushes up with his arms delivering a rising kick to Hawkins's face. Hawkins staggers back slightly as Katz twirls around rising back to his feet he leaps forward smashing his fist across Hawkins head. Hawkins steps back again dazed slightly from the blow he shakes it off. He looks at Katz, seeing him standing across the field with one open palm facing towards him.

Hawkins rolls his shoulders looking at Katz, "Have you improved your atomic energy as well? Let's see what is greater my spite, or your powers."

Hawkins's muscles begin to bulge as he grows bigger towering over his opponent. Katz focuses as a red sphere builds in front of his palm. The energy from the sphere begins to create waves of heat through the air as the sphere flashes yellow and orange. Katz raises one eyebrow quickly before unleashing a massive blast of atomic energy. The beam rushes towards Hawkins at amazing speeds slamming directly into his left hand, which he uses to block it. Hawkins is pushed back from the beam as it engulfs his entire hand rolling over his arm and up his shoulder. The rest of Hawkins's body is covered in the blast as a large explosion rocks the projects destroying the buildings within the radius of the attack.

A chaotic burning wind passes by in the night sky blowing Katz's crown from his head as he stands near the center of the explosion completely unscathed. Katz looks around for a quick second before shrugging, he then turns preparing to take off when a large shadow appears behind him, towering over Katz the shadow reaches out grappling him with a bear hug, Hawkins lifts him high before jumping from the cloud of flames and debris.

Katz turns back looking at Hawkins his jaw drops, "How did you survive that!?"

Hawkins continues to climb upwards tightly holding Katz, he squeezes cracking parts of his armor. "Katz you know my skin is nigh impervious even to your blast but that did burn...I will make you suffer for it." Katz squints as Hawkins flips him over diving towards the ground at high speeds he prepares to drive Katz's head into the earth.

Katz closes his eyes as the wind begins to whistle around him he thinks to himself, "Well crap...this is going to break my neck...unless...."

The two freeze in the air descending at slow speeds as Sentry flies over grabbing Katz he pulls him back into regular time. "Got you boss, I know you said to go on ahead, but I was worried so I waited and was watching."

Katz wriggles free with the help of Sentry as the two move away from Hawkins. "Good job, I didn't really need your help but I'll take it. Shall I assume Arcos and Titallic already went to eat?"

Sentry nods, "Yes boss Arcos was especially hungry today."

Katz rolls his eyes, "Well hmm…I was hoping to get through to Hawkins right now but maybe we shall save it for later. How long does your time abilities last anyway?"

Sentry responds, "Well I can probably hold him there for another minute or two at most but he is heavy…."

Katz bobs his head around, "Good enough let's go eat!"

The two rocket off leaving Hawkins to continue his slow descent for another two minutes before he falls out of the time lock and slams into the ground below.

Chapter 3: Military Attack

Back in Chicago, Brainstorm and the other heroes head back to a high rise apartment complex. Flying over to the building they arrive at a penthouse suite landing on the porch, they step through the sliding glass doors tired and dirty. Inside they are greeted by a middle age man with short brown and blond hair his dark eyes comb over their damaged clothing and ruined suits as he shakes his head. "I guess everything didn't go so well out in the field today?"

Brainstorm shakes his head, "No Monos, no. Brutilus, or 'em Hawkins escaped and we got trashed by Katz's band again. It would have helped if you were there."

Monos strolls over to the TV turning on the news he watches a recap of the day. "I should have been there but I just had other things to do. I was meeting with a mercenary. He said he could help us for the right price. I had to go and get the money from my account and all."

Landlord shrugs going off to the back rooms he heads to his room to clean up. Brainstorm responds, "You know we don't have much left in the way of funds for this, who is this mercenary anyway? Now Monos that is a pretty sad excuse for not showing up."

Monos pulls up a picture on his phone, "Ralph is his name and he is from Kansas. We defeated him a few months back and sent him to jail, but the government found him to be more useful as a tactical weapon. He of course didn't find that to his liking after the pay dried up and left. He stays down the street and his powers are definitely something we can use to our advantage."

Tyreal chimes in, "Wasn't he the one with gravity powers? That dude was sick; he almost flattened a city! How did you know he was here?!"

Monos turns to Tyreal, "I have a knack for those things don't worry about that. He will be an invaluable resource though."

Tyreal squints, "In other words Brainstorm found him, well you are the leader Monos so whatever you say goes. I just hope he doesn't betray us or anything like that."

Monos chuckles, "No that is doubtful he seems to be honorable when he is being paid, I'll monitor the situation though. I did invite him over for our planning session he should be here shortly."

Landlord returns in a sleek tan suit cleaned off with bandages over his wounds he sits down on the couch. "So what did I miss?"

The doorbell rings as Monos smirks, "You're about to see actually." He walks over opening the door before them stands a young man with spiked hair and a small pointed nose. His brown eyebrows point upwards while he runs his finger through his hair. Taking off his biker jacket he hands it to Monos while walking in the door. His pointed black goatee sticks out from his chin as he jumps over the couch sitting down in front of the TV.

He looks around the room quickly before returning his attention to the TV. "So what are we doing dudes?"

The rest of the heroes stand completely confused and baffled while Monos hangs up the jacket, "This is Ralph for any of you that have forgotten."

"That's my name," Ralph says with a smirk.

Katz and Sentry arrive at Joseph's restaurant a large overhang leads the way up to the fancy wooden doors. A long red carpet runs out to the sidewalk as a strong yellow light beams out of the doorway, silence fills the air as Katz and Sentry stroll through the double doors entering the restaurant they find a crowd of people sitting completely still they quietly eat their food while glancing over at a long table in the back. One of the customers screams as she sees Katz walk in with Sentry. From the back an arm waves them over. Katz and Sentry walk pass the crowd feeling the fear surrounding them they step to the long table in the back to find Arcos and Titallic devouring plates of food.

Katz and Sentry sit down at the table while a waiter brings over glasses of water hastily. Heavy beads of sweat fall down his forehead landing on his vest as he shivers. Katz rolls his eyes over to him, "You don't need to worry child…I'm not in the disintegrating mood tonight. Please tell Joseph I would like the pepperoni and pineapple pizza tonight and that he better deliver it himself, unless he doesn't mind losing another one of his staff."

"Um…ya…ya…yes sir…right on it…sir…yes," stampers the waiter as he moves on to Sentry.

Sentry waves his hand, "the usual," leaving the waiter to quickly rush off to the kitchen.

Arcos cleans off the last chunk of steak from his plate rubbing his stomach he sits back putting his feet up on the table. "This is the life boss, about time we got a good meal in. How did it go with Hawkins?"

Katz takes a sip from his glass, "Well there is no good news actually…our base has been ruined which simply means we need to ramp up the completion of the tower; and I couldn't get Hawkins to do anything aside from try to kill me. All is not lost though thanks to Sentry I'm still fine."

Arcos pitches one of Titallic's chicken wings at Katz but Katz catches it with a fork easily placing it down on the table. "What is that boss? We don't have a home anymore and the only thing you have to say is that you are still fine! I think it is time for a change in leadership, so far all you have done is ruined our home and had us runaway from killing your old buddies. I say we take this country and the world by storm and rule it with an iron fist!"

Katz chuckles, "Oh all ways the impetuous one aren't you now Arcos, you never could see the way my plans are perfectly aligned."

Sentry looks over at both of them, "But boss Arcos does have a small point the more time we waste trying to build that tower and all, the more time the government and Brainstorm has to find ways to defeat us. Why don't we just kill them all? I know we could do it easily."

Katz picks up his glass churning the water in a spiral he bobs his head around in thought, "I have told you all before that the government wronged me. I haven't told you the details about that, just know that they did it. As such my plan is not one of true conquest in the warrior taking over sense. But in the sense of fear, manipulation, and the view of control. Think about it; whenever you all go out there and defeat those worthless individuals how are you viewed?

"Does terror fill the souls of the mortals amongst us? Look at this restaurant for instance, this is power. We hold them hostage not in the physical sense, but in a more psychological capacity. And once that capacity reaches its max then, and only then can we strike at the government. Then can we destroy them and have the people fall under us completely. I don't need any government, person, or group thinking that there is hope for them. If that hope is constantly beaten down, but not killed how much easier is it to control and manipulate people? They are like lemmings, or other foolish animals, once their symbols have been broken so too will they."

Katz shifts his eyes back to Arcos with a nod he glances at Arcos's eyes seeing a glint of anger in them he shrugs. "Now then my boys after we are done here we will be shipping out to Los Angeles it's about time the second in, command took well, command.

Arcos finishes his cup of soda wiping his mouth a large grin appears on his face, "Absolutely boss that will do."

Katz looks over to the side seeing one of the waiters on the phone he rolls his eyes.

A moment later a bald man scurries out of the backroom carrying two trays of food he hustles over to Katz and the others. His head glows red with nervousness as he sets the trays down on the table sliding the food across to each member of Katz's team. The man then rushes over to Katz's side bowing down and trembling he pleads with him.

Katz starts looking mildly annoyed, "What do you want this time Joseph? We bring you business and you return it with this shivering and fear; have we killed you yet? No I didn't think so get up."

"Um…ah…sir…I just wanted to ask and I hope you take no offense to this but…why me…why my livelihood and my restaurant? I was just getting back on track, people started coming here again and you all show up now, I'll be ruined."

Katz growls, "Joseph you act like we don't do you a service of keeping your establishment safe from thieves and mobsters. We come here because the pizza is good and the other food is probably tasty too. But I will admit you have upset me today."

Joseph's eyes grow wide with shock, "How so…sir…how so is the food not perfect?"

Katz bites down on a slice of pizza chewing it slowly he swallows with the most pleased look on his face, "Nope it is the same as always…but your little waiter friend that went on that phone earlier…who do you think he was talking too umm?"

Joseph's jaw drops, "Dr. Katz if I may call you that sir…"

"You may," Katz says interrupting Joseph.

"Well umm you see the alarm was tripped when your friends arrived, the waiter was calling to tell them everything was fine." Katz and his team laugh at the excuse while the sound of multiple vehicles can be heard rummaging through the street outside.

Katz gets up followed by the rest of his team as they pass through the main restaurant towards the door. He turns back looking directly at Joseph, "If I bleed…you will bleed." Joseph faints while Katz and his team step out the open front doors to see an array of military vehicles and soldiers outside the restaurant aiming directly at them.

"Freeze you terrorist are all to be detained, surrender now we have you surrounded!" Yells one of the captains standing at the machine gun of a tank with its sights set directly on the group.

Katz yawns covering his mouth, he then crosses his arms and takes a step forward into the street. The sound of guns cocking and weapons being loaded resounds through the street as Katz stops, gazing over the wall of soldiers in his path.

"I will not tell you again we will open fire!"

Behind the group the waiters and waitresses close the doors, locking them they gathering the customers in the back. Titallic looks around waiting for a signal while Katz continues to count the numbers of his enemies.

Katz opens his mouth, "Now then let's see you all have quite a force here, did you bring enough body bags for the death toll as well hmm? Well leader of these brave men and women…are you ready to sacrifice all of their lives?"

The captain swallows a tough lump in his throat as he shakes his head, "We won't die you will! We would rather not destroy American property so I ask you again stand down! This is your final warning!"

Katz responds quickly, "And I'd rather not have you ruin one of my favorite restaurants with your brazen shooting and shelling. Therefore this is how we will do this…follow me if you can."

The four characters jump into the air flying several blocks down the road they land in a park. The military group turns and opens fire while chasing after them. Katz looks to Titallic giving him a nod he takes a step back. Titallic smirks stepping forward his body begins to glow and mutate growing larger as his skin begins to transform into metal.

The barrage of bullets bounces off Titallic striking the buildings and deflecting into the streets as he walks forward towards the troops. A single bullet ricochets off of Titallic and bounces back killing one of the soldiers instantly. An APC runs down the road ramming into Titallic, but he grabs the vehicle. The two slide down the road slightly until Titallic plants his feet firmly into the ground lifting the APC off the road he smashes it into the side of a building. The vehicle explodes as a discharge of electricity runs down Titallic's arm.

Smoke billows in front of Titallic as a loud boom is heard through the smoke and fire; a tank shell smashes into Titallic's chest launching him through the air and pass Katz, who sways to the side avoiding the metal man. A medium size tank rolls through the smoke leading the charge with the soldiers and other vehicles behind it. Titallic sits up holding his chest in pain while Katz shakes his head.

Arcos steps in as tank takes aim preparing to fire again. He stands firm staring down the barrel of the machine he lifts one finger towards it. The controls begin to go haywire short circuiting and exploding in front of the soldier as the tank begins to spin out of control. The cannon turns backwards towards another tank as the shell is released booming through the air, the tank shell rips through the other vehicle.

The explosion and debris from the destroyed tank slam into the soldiers surrounding it killing them. Arcos then snaps his fingers causing the first tank to explode blowing one of the soldiers out of the hatch. Twin rockets come down from the buildings above, exploding next to Arcos as he shields his eyes from the heat. Two soldiers slide up on the ground taking aim they unleash a storm of bullets at Arcos, but the bullets barely sting his skin falling on the ground harmless.

Sentry jumps off the ground rising high he grabs one of the rocket soldiers, tossing the soldier off the building. The other soldier takes up her RPG aiming at Sentry she fires. The rocket flies pass the building and into the clouds she takes her eye out of the scope looking around shocked. "Well where did he go…?"

Sentry taps her on the shoulder, as she turns around she reaches for her sidearm only to be punched in the gut she falls unconscious. On the rooftop Sentry turns his attention to Arcos as the air around him grows hot, he vanishes again teleporting over to Arcos he grabs him and teleports back behind Katz.

Titallic walks over looking to Katz, "Well boss what do ya want to do about the lot of them? I kind of want to get back to eating."

"Not to worry I'm about to end it now…should I try to leave one of them alive…maybe so…here we go." Katz says as he claps his hands together slowly pulling them apart, he amasses a large amount of atomic energy between his palms. The captain rolls up with his tank, taking the lead they take aim firing off a shell. Katz slams his hands together with a loud clap the atomic energy bolts out from his palms in a straight beam it disintegrates the shell as it rushes pass, running over the military forces it melts the tanks and kills most of the soldiers turning them to ash.

The bright light from the atomic energy illuminates the area as Katz lowers his hands yawning. "That's twice in one day I've had to use my powers in such a fashion. This is draining."

"Boss you need to rest you know your abilities are costly." Sentry says with concern in his voice. "Let's go to Albert's place."

Katz shrugs in an attempt to look tough, "We only need 2 hours of sleep a day anyway, but I will admit they are a little taxing…a little taxing though."

A bullet rings out hitting Katz in the head as one of the soldiers crawls forward severely burned and bleeding he fires another bullet off. The bullet is caught by Katz as he holds it in his hand he shakes his head tossing it to the ground. Katz raises one finger aiming it at the gun he immediately disintegrates it.

He turns towards his group, "Well now that we have settled that account dinner for the remainder of the night has been cancelled. We will eat again at some point, but for now let's leave these humans to their own devices and head towards LA."

The soldier tries to get up, suffering greatly from the burns, but he passes out in a pool of his own blood. Katz and the others take to the air rising high above the buildings they figure their location before rocketing off into the distance.

The next day the soldier awakens in a medical facility the bright lights nearly blind him as he tries to look around the room. His body is covered in bandages as he lays hooked up to a machine. General Neisse walks in his broad shoulders covering most of the door as the doctor comes in after him.

Neisse looks over his patient files with the shake of his head he tosses them back down on the desk. "Well soldier Gamaden you did a commendable job last night, although the majority of your unit was killed without a trace left. But we are graced by your return, and that of Melancole, of course none of this is of any real help against the threat that plagues our entire way of life! So soldier do you have anything to add to the conversation!?"

Gamaden motions to respond but the doctor stands between him and Neisse, "General sir he is my patient first once he is healed up then you can speak to him. Until then there is nothing to be gained from this harassment, and I will not tolerate it on my watch." Neisse sucks his teeth in annoyance before walking out of the room. He heads down a hallway and onto the elevator. Arriving at the bottom floor Neisse takes up his phone.

A soft buzz can be heard as Wizencut picks up his cell looking at it he shakes his head, "Yes Niesse any news?"

Niesse punches the wall, "What do you think!? I know you saw that news report this morning we lost 89 people last night....89 is Washington still taking this lightly? Every time we get into a fight with them we die…and they do nothing about it! This can't go on."

Wizencut places his hand on his forehead, "Neisse what have I told you about that tone and voice with me. Regardless President Roy has seen the latest and has approved the use of more lethal force. Air support and other weapons are on the way right now. I'll be back within the next few days, so I would suggest you keep calm and take a break from hunting for a while."

Wizencut ends the call leaving Niesse speechless on the other line. Niesse smirks for a second before stepping out of the building while dark clouds build over the city.

Chapter 4: Turning Tides

Katz and the others soar over the Los Angeles border looking over at his wrist band he finds a message from Albert. "We will be meeting him at the park across from his place try not to give him a hard time Arcos."

Arcos rolls his eyes as the four descend over the city. A number of citizens see the crew flying around the buildings. Looking on in terror they begin to run away from the area. The group lands in a large open park in the distance children play on an old swing set and adults can be seen running with their dogs and friends. A middle aged blond haired man gets off the bench folding up his newspaper he tucks it under his arm against his dark blue shirt. His blue eyes shimmer in the morning light as a dog runs around next to him.

The man walks over to Katz standing over him he gives Katz a hug. "He bud how have you been? It has been a while since you came to visit."

Katz nods, "Albert Alberason yeah it has been a while but I'm well. The boys have been doing well, but they still need some work."

Albert replies, "Well that's to be expected. I saw you guys on the news actually good job back in Chicago last night. I'm surprised the military and law enforcement even tries anymore."

Sentry laughs, "Boss killed so many last night it was amazing."

Katz shrugs, "I try not brag too much about that. Albert we have come here not simply for a reunion. Hawkins stopped by at the secret base no less."

Albert stares shocked, "He knows where it is?!"

Katz sighs, "He knew where it was then he decided to level it. The home that we had for a year is now gone."

Arcos spits on the ground, "It was a shack in the projects we could have had much better if we weren't wasting our time hiding."

Albert walks over to Arcos extending his hand but Arcos crosses his arms in defiance. "I'm not here to be your buddy Albert like everyone else; we need to get this show on the road."

"I see that Arcos," Albert says, "Doesn't matter though we will get though that thick skull of yours soon enough."

Albert turns away from Arcos returning his attention to Katz and the others he points them in the direction of his home. The five men walk down a path coming to the end of the park they stand before a tall apartment building. Albert leads them in and up to the second floor as the other tenants peek out seeing Katz and the others they quickly shut their doors or run out of the building. A couple call the police but they refuse any service as Albert opens the door to a large apartment filled with numerous metal spears and spikes along the walls. As they walk towards the center of the apartment several pathways lead off in various directions.

Albert points around the apartment, "Alright extra rooms are down on your left and right. The kitchen is ahead and the living room is to the right and then left. I'll go and get you all something to eat."

Katz shakes his hand, "No need to do that Albert we already ate. We won't need food for a good while. I think we will instead just rest for a little bit after we get cleaned up."

Albert shrugs, "Alright that's fine by me." I'll see you guys in a couple of hours then."

As Katz retires to his room Arcos sneaks over to Titallic finding him sitting on his bed. Arcos stands at the door closing it behind him he turns his eyes towards Titallic. "What do you want Arcos?"

Arcos walks over to the window peeking out on the city he folds his arms behind his back. "Titallic how long have we been at this? A year now or so since the world really saw us and since our first battle with those idiots Brainstorm and his ilk and what have we to show for it? We are now stuck up in an apartment, a nice one at that, but nonetheless an apartment in LA when we should already have the world bowing down at our feet."

Titallic falls flat on the bed resting his head in the pillow he smiles with comfort. "Yeah I can see what you're saying. People are afraid of us though you saw that from the restaurant and it isn't like the military can really do anything to us. Though it would be nice to finally be rid of Brainstorm and friends if you know what I mean."

Arcos smirks, "Exactly and you know what we never will be rid of them. You know Katz, he use to work with them."

Titallic shifts his brown eyes over to Arcos, "Yeah I know I was the first recruit after Albert I know all about the backstory and everything, or at least everything he has told us...."

Arcos responds, "Which means that he won't kill them! He has a soft spot you can see it in his eyes whenever I bring up slaughtering the ingrates he always says in time. Even when we go out on missions to kill them he always calls us back or sets the goal for something else when they are right there in front of us.

"You know he use to work with them, him and Albert. Those two started it all with Monos and Brainstorm. I will never forget seeing what they did to petty criminals in Chicago last year. He told me himself when he recruited me This is how I know he will never do what is needed and rid the world of them."

Titallic shrugs, "What do you want me to do about it then Arcos? I'm not about to bring a suggestion to the boss he knows what he is doing supposedly."

A smirk crawls across Arcos's face as he turns to Titallic, "Who said anything about suggestions. Who said he had to be the leader?"

Titallic sits up looking slightly curious he rubs his chin, "What are you suggesting a mutiny haha and we would all follow you?"

Arcos snaps, "Exactly I already have a plan to deal with him and Albert if he continues to fight at Katz's side. All you have to do is join me it will be fun; we don't even have to kill the boss we just have to show him that I was right all along."

Titallic starts, "And what makes you think I won't go and tell him this right now?"

Arcos says, "He wouldn't take it seriously even if you did and because you know I'm right. This whole build a tower to rule the world idea is stupid. It makes absolutely no sense we have the power with or without the damn tower!"

Instantly Sentry teleports into the room shocking both Titallic and Arcos as Arcos stares looking completely dumbfounded. "Hmm...you know you're lucky boss is down on the other side of the building...it may not have ended well for you had he heard you just now."

Arcos squints at Sentry while looking around the room for a potential weapon, "So you heard it all then? And what do you think?"

Sentry responds, "I heard what I needed to hear and I'll go along with it as long as boss and Albert aren't killed. I'm tired of living in a shack and getting so close to killing Tyreal only to be pulled back. But I suppose that depends on your plan." Arcos smirks once again as he begins to lay out the plan to them.

Later that day Katz rises from his bed, stretching he walks over to his armor. Looking over the cracks along the side left from Hawkins he squints before kneeling down repairing the fractures with the atomic energy at his fingertips. As he steps outside of his room and walks down to the living room he finds Albert sitting outside on the balcony.

"Well Albert what have you been up to since our last meeting?" Katz says as he steps through the sliding doors and hangs over the balcony looking down.

Albert smiles, "To be honest with you I've been stealing the parts that we need for the tower and dating this amazing girl Emily. We have really had a great time together and we are talking about marriage Katz."

Katz's eyes twitch for a second as he turns his head back to Albert, "What…what…what. Amazing is right Albert and why have you not told me of this beforehand? When is the wedding let's go and steal stuff to make it grand."

Albert rubs his nose with a grin on his face, "Haha I wasn't exactly sure it was even going to happen, I haven't even proposed yet so we still have a ways to go. Besides you are busy and I didn't want to add anymore to your plate."

Katz waves his hand, "Pish posh Albert you know I always have time for you all. Which reminds me Arcos is getting a little unruly wouldn't you say?"

Albert raises his eyebrows in reassurance, "Katz I have said it before and I'll say it again, you are far too soft on those boys."

Katz laughs, "How so?"

Albert continues, "You can see it in their eyes that they are itching for blood that you won't let them have. It's like teasing a dog with food eventually it will bite and I don't know how well you would fair against a bite like that with your frail skin."

Katz bobs his head around, "Ahh but that is why I have this barrier of atomic energy around it is constant and quite durable. Besides even if he revolts against me, and even by chance if the others do I can take them all."

Albert tosses Katz a surprised look, "Can you really say that with 100% confidence? Cause I can see that they aren't the same as they were a year ago. They have all gotten much better at what they do; remember when Sentry couldn't even stop time around you? I'm pretty sure he could freeze you instantly at any given moment."

Katz shifts his eyes around with a puzzled look before responding, "Umm…yeah…he probably could in fact I'm almost certain he can. But to be honest with you I doubt that he would do that they are all pretty loyal, Arcos is just trying to test his boundaries to see how far he can push it. He knows what will happen if he pushes too far."

Looking unsure Albert says, "Still you put far too much faith in them, they are human after all and we know how you feel about them."

Katz eyes grow sharp, "You have a small point but that is all. I know them well and they wouldn't do anything. Regardless I will take your advice into consideration on to more important things though. Will you return to Chicago with us? We have a bit of work to do on the tower before it is finished and we could use the help bashing in those military and Brainstorm's gang."

Albert stands up taking in a breath of air he shakes Katz's hand. "Alright we will handle this, just let me tell Emily and see what she says. Also of note Katz, what about Brainstorm and Monos?"

Katz shrugs, "What about them?"

Albert responds, "Is that the reason you haven't had the boys kill them yet? You still feel a little sentimental about it? I mean they had you completely wrapped around their fingers. It isn't hard to imagine that being the reason they are still alive. You just don't want to kill them do you?"

Katz grumbles, "Alberason…don't cross me. Those two need to die…but you have a point I am still fond of them…enough not to kill them…of course that could also be because I don't see them often."

Albert responds, "As you say Katz. Just don't let it get to you. And don't let the others see it, then they will really mutiny against you."

Katz walks back inside noticing the peculiar silence in the apartment he walks down the other wing to find his team. As enters one of the rooms he finds a piece of paper sitting on the bed picking it up he glances over the words as his eyes grow wide with shock. He turns out of the room and strolls back to Albert, "You go and take care of you thing with Emily. It would seem my boys are getting out of hand as you so said. They went back to town and left me a note…."

"They couldn't have gotten too far, how did they sneak out though is the question." Albert says with a puzzled look.

Katz squints, "That Sentry and his teleporting that's how…or he might have slowed down time and left with them. Regardless none of that matters. I'll go and take care of this, you can follow along later."

Katz takes off from the balcony flying quickly he heads East towards Chicago while Albert shakes his head, "This won't end well."

Chapter 5: Siege

Back in Chicago Arcos and the others descend on the city they land next to the Willis Tower creating a huge scene in front of the people. Titallic steps forward shooting out multiple electric bolts striking the cars causing numerous explosions over the area. Arcos runs over grabbing a car he lifts it off the ground tossing it into the building across the street. Sirens blare as the police speed over to the area along with the SWAT teams. They line up along the cross streets, each officer looking extremely nervous as they take aim with their guns. One of the Sheriffs gets up raising her loud speaker she takes a deep breath. As she starts to speak an electric bolt rips through her car door knocking her over.

"No, no, no little missy, you will be silent." Titallic then stabs his hands into the ground sending heavy electric waves along the road shocking the officers.

Niesse gets up from his office walking down the hall to the command room he looks at the surveillance camera watching the destruction he grits his teeth in annoyance. "They need to hurry up with my aid."

Arcos looks over the destruction crossing his arms he laughs, "This is great about time we let loose."

Sentry shakes his head, "You ready for when they get here?"

Arcos nods, "Of course kill them all, this time no holding back."

News choppers circle around the area showing the destruction to the world. Outside of their penthouse the heroes jump off, heading out quickly they fly towards the tower at high speeds.

Walking through a mall Hawkins stops in front of the electronics seeing the attack on the news he rubs his beard before tilting his hat down, he walks out of the store.

"This time Katz you won't escape me so easily." Hawkins says as he heads down the road towards the Willis tower.

Sentry walks over to a police car under a storm of bullet fire he grabs the car lifting it above his head he prepares to smash the officers when suddenly a psychic blast slams into his chest sending Sentry barreling back.

Titallic catches him as his body transforms into metal he looks up to see Monos and the others flying towards them. "Got what you wanted Arcos…? There are five of them…wait…what…five….?"

"I thought there was only four actual fighters still… it doesn't matter, we can kill another one." Arcos says with a smile.

The three villains take off from the ground rushing upwards they split up dashing in from the sides. Monos stops allowing the others to fly forth Brainstorm bursts ahead striking Sentry across the face with a mighty kick. Sentry's jaw cracks as he is thrust through the sky and into the tower. Lightning ripples down from above rushing into the tower the bolt hits Sentry pushing him out the other side of the building and onto a rooftop. Sentry gets up surprised by Brainstorm's power as he gazes up his foe pounces over him delivering a flurry of punches and kicks.

Sentry quickly snaps both fingers stopping time and Brainstorm. He jumps back as time resumes and Brainstorm stops his attack seeing Sentry standing back from him. Sentry rushes in within that second throwing a solid punch towards Brainstorm. But his adversary grabs his arm pushing it upward he steps in with an elbow ready. Sentry stops his elbow with an open palm pushing back with all his might he staggers Brainstorm.

Within that moment Sentry steps forward attacking Brainstorm with a straight followed up with an uppercut. He twirls around hitting Brainstorm in the face with a rising kick sending him up into the sky. Brainstorm flips over catching himself he lifts one hand towards the sky calling forth a stream of hail. Sentry jumps around dodging the large icy rocks. He then teleports behind Brainstorm attempting to land a drop kick. Sentry's body bounces off a psychic barrier around his foe. Brainstorm releases a pulse of psychic energy, flowing from the barrier; it strikes Sentry again pushing him across town and into another rooftop.

Titallic sends out two electric blasts at Tyreal and Ralph. Ralph sways to the side easily while Tyreal takes the attack head on blocking it. Seeing his attack fail he rushes in blitzing Tyreal with a barrage of hard metal punches and kicks. The blows smash into Tyreal with tremendous force, sending him crashing to the ground. The asphalt breaks under the force of Tyreal's body as Titallic turns his attention to Ralph. "Who are you?"

Ralph spins a coin between his fingers looking at Titallic with a smirk, "Ralph's the name dude, and I work for money…you got some?"

Titallic gives Ralph a confused look, "None for you but I'll take your life anyway."

Ralph shrugs, "We'll see about that." Ralph unfolds his hands letting them drop to his sides he floats still in the air. Titallic speeds forward going in for another blitz, but he suddenly feels his body growing heavy. He attempts to stay in the air but he is pulled down to the ground with tremendous force and weight. Titallic then struggles to get up pushing against the ground with all his strength but he falls flat on his face.

Ralph drops down with a few drops of sweat falling from his brow; he holds both hands out towards Titallic. "Haha holding you here is proving to be a bit more of a challenge than I first anticipated, but even you for all your strength can do nothing against me. Once I'm done flattening you, I'll take care of the others too."

Titallic barely tilts his head far enough to look up at Ralph he then closes his eyes calling down a lightning strike on Ralph. Ralph shouts in pain breaking his focus and allowing Titallic to leap up hammering Ralph with a heavy punch to the gut. Ralph's eyes become massive as he is thrown backwards blasting through three buildings and rolling into a park.

Titallic breathes heavily when Tyreal comes up from behind him entangling him in a slew of chains. Tyreal lifts Titallic into the air slamming him down multiple times before jumping up and kicking Titallic in the chest. Numerous metal spears rise from the edge of Tyreal's chains scratching against Titallic's armored body while Tyreal disappears in a puff of smoke. Titallic regains his balance, looking around for Tyreal he finds nothing until Tyreal comes down from above, his hand covered in green energy; he strikes Titallic in the back with a hard energized punch forcing Titallic through a skyscraper cutting the building in two.

Arcos flips through the air throwing two kicks at Landlord who easily dodges to the side. Landlord grabs Arcos by the leg swinging him around; he tosses Arcos towards the Willis building. Arcos spins through the air landing on his feet he pushes off the building to build up speed tackling Landlord through the sky and into a school. The two crash and roll through the classrooms landing in a computer room. Landlord kicks Arcos back while getting to his feet, but Arcos uses two of his fingers to direct the machines exploding the two computers next to Landlord.

While Landlord is stunned Arcos charges forward grabbing a chair he swings it with his full strength smashing it across Landlord's face. Landlord is sent spiraling through a wall and onto the playground, Arcos steps through the hole with a smile. Landlord punches both of his fists into the ground waiting patiently for Arcos he sits still. Suddenly the school and the grounds around it begin to shake with terror causing Arcos to stumble slightly before he takes to the air hovering over the land.

Arcos taunts, "Come on Landlord, we all know your powers are worthless just like you. I'm going to enjoy ripping off your head."

Arcos speeds over the land heading for Landlord with a bloodthirsty look in his eyes. As he approaches Landlord pulls his hands from the ground causing the earth under Arcos to shoot up in large clumps of rock. The heavy rocks strike Arcos pushing him upwards as more rocks and boulders rise up around him. Arcos gets up in an attempt to jump off the rock when another boulder swings into him knocking him back. The other rocks swirl around him building a cage before dropping him to the ground. The prison of rock stops in front of Landlord who snaps his fingers, encasing the rock with vines tightening its hold over Arcos.

Arcos attempts to call a vehicle over to him but his signal fails to get through the thick layers of rock, as Landlord stands in front of him with a smirk on his face. "We got you all this time!" Arcos punches against the rock breaking through it he finds another boulder mounting on top of it.

Arcos grumbles, "Damn! What did you all do?"

Landlord smirks, "We know you all are strong but that doesn't mean that we can't pair off to deal with you guys. Sentry's powers have always been too much for Tyreal, but Brainstorm can constantly hold a barrier around him blocking all of his attacks. Ralph was the secret weapon against Titallic, and trapping you so you couldn't send signals to machines was my task. We beat you all now surrender!"

Arcos cocks on eyebrow to the side, "So you think." Stepping back Arcos holding out his arm he prepares his cannon to fire as the energy builds up vines stretch through the rock and onto Arcos's gun.

The vines rush into the energy veins as Arcos quickly detaches the weapon, suddenly a side of the rock prison is blown away as the cannon fires. Arcos quickly jumps out with only seconds to spare as the gun overloads and explodes. He turns towards Landlord with hate in his eyes; he lunges over the field tackling Landlord to the ground. Arcos then wraps his hands around Landlord's neck in an attempt to choke him to death.

Landlord kicks Arcos off scratching his head he looks at him, "What were you trying to do suffocate me…? You know how long that would take with as little as I need to breathe?" Arcos grumbles before jumping into the air taking off at full speed he looks around seeing Sentry falling through the sky he flies over to him helping him off the ground.

"This isn't going as planned Arcos…." Sentry says while holding his side, "We need some better options."

Arcos nods, "It will get better, just give me a minute we need to get to Titallic and stay together it is our best bet."

Sentry nods, "I saw Titallic being run through a building a little ways from here hold on." Sentry jumps teleporting across the land with Arcos, they appear at the side of the collapsing building. Looking around they find Titallic pulling himself from the rubble, his metal body still shinning and barely scratched.

Titallic jogs over to Sentry and Arcos, "Guys this is dumb. That Ralph guy the gravity guy….he is annoying like none other."

Arcos shakes his head, "We have to stick together and take them on as one this is an uphill battle."

Monos descends before them followed by the rest of the heroes, they stand across from the villains with their arms crossed. Monos's eyes begin to turn grey as his hair bobs in the wind. "This is your last chance to surrender before I make you."

Arcos steps forward with a brave face, "Haha you can't do anything Monos we know all about your powers you are weak just like Katz was back then there is no way."

Monos shakes his head, "You have forced my hand. I didn't want to do it this way but you leave me no options." Monos's hair stands on end as he raises one arm towards the villains.

Arcos smirks feeling nothing he prepares to attack when suddenly he falls, to his knees grabbing his throbbing head he yells in pain. The others collapse as well breathing heavily they struggle to move. Monos's hair begins to turn grey; while inside the villain's minds their emotions are slowly churned showing them their darkest demons. Weakness fills their bodies as their emotions run haywire nearly driving them insane.

Brainstorm calls down three bolts of lightning electrocuting the villains and knocking them unconscious. Monos drops to the ground taking a breath he focuses his mind as his hair returns to its blond color.

Brainstorm helps Monos to his feet taking one hand he traps the three in a psychic bubble. "Monos you did it!"

Monos holds his chest in slight pain as he looks around at the damage, "I should have done more sooner."

Tyreal walks over looking at the bubble he crosses his arms, "You know, we can use them as bait to catch the real mastermind Katz."

Brainstorm smirks, "We can move them over the water and hold them there. That way Katz will be drawn out to an area where he has no cover and can't use people as a defense. It will be the best way to end everything, and then all we will have to worry about is Hawkins."

Brainstorm lifts the bubble as he floats slightly off the ground. "Well what do you think Monos?"

Monos reponds, "Alright we need to bring closure to this before it gets more out of hand. We'll set them up on a pillar and keep the barrier around I'll deal with Katz when he gets here." The others hover into the air following Brainstorm they head towards Lake Michigan. As they near the shore a car spirals through the sky slamming into Landlord it knocks him out of the air. Landlord skids across the road and crashes into a boat the group looks around to see Hawkins standing firm on the ground s

ing up at them.

Hawkins removes his coat taking off his glasses and his hat he rotates his shoulders. "You aren't taking them anywhere. I need them to get to Katz, and I'll take them from you if I have to."

Hawkins's eyes turn red as his armored undershirt expands with his muscles. His body enlarges as his skin turns red. Tyreal attempts to restrict Hawkins with numerous binding chains but each chain shatters as Hawkins completes his transformation.

He jumps at amazing speeds grabbing Tyreal by the face; he drops down slamming him head first into a rooftop. Brainstorm sets the villains down on the shore, flying after Hawkins along with Monos the two speed around him in an attempt to flank Hawkins. Brainstorm strikes with a spinning kick but Hawkins grabs his leg turning around he smashes Brainstorm into Monos with one mighty swing. The two roll through the air crashing into the harbor, while Hawkins kicks Tyreal off the rooftop and onto the road below.

He then turns his attention towards the villains walking towards them steadily. Monos gets up flying to Hawkins he stops in front of him. "You aren't taking them and you should surrender yourself!"

Hawkins laughs hysterically, "You think that I would be beaten by you little Monos the man who couldn't tame Katz. I will break you if you get in my way."

Monos remains firm in a defensive stance as Hawkins charges forward throwing a heavy punch. Monos steps to the side, sensing Hawkins's emotions he jumps about dodging each of the blows with ease. He steps forward jumping Monos hits Hawkins with a flying kick pushing him back. Hawkins tries to grab Monos, but he slips under his hands pushing off the ground he strikes upward with another kick to Hawkins's chest. Hawkins is launched into the air from the blow while Monos flips over charging after his enemy. Hawkins pulls his hands back swinging them forward with massive force he claps them together sending out a large shockwave.

The wave smashes into Monos sending him spiraling towards the ground; Hawkins charges after him planting both feet firmly onto Monos's chest he flattens him into the ground. Monos yells in pain under the weight of Hawkins as Landlord pulls himself the wreckage of the boat, running quickly he jumps after Hawkins tackling him off of Monos the two roll across the street. Landlord leaps off of Hawkins lifting one hand up he entombs Hawkins in a mound of earth and concrete. Clapping his hands together Landlord forces the mound to twist and contort squeezing Hawkins, but Hawkins pushes against the walls breaking through the earth he smashes the mound freeing himself.

Landlord covers his hands with hard rocks, he runs forward throwing punches at Hawkins, but he counters each blow shattering the rock shell and hammering Landlord in the gut with a hard right. Hawkins then steps forward driving his foot into Landlord's chest. Landlord rockets back crashing through a light pole and slamming into a semi-truck.

The truck explodes blowing Landlord out onto the road. He crawls across in an attempt to get to his feet. Hawkins returns to his objective jumping high he arrives on the shore looking over the unconscious bodies of the three villains. He takes a single step forward but he runs into a psychic wall blocking him. Brainstorm descends to the front, holding up the wall he wraps it around Hawkins.

Ralph floats over to Monos hovering over him he cocks his head to the side, "Well looks like you got beat up dude."

Monos struggles pulling himself from the ground he barely gets up, "Ahh…aren't you helping Ralph?"

Ralph raises an eyebrow in disgust, "I think I did what I was paid for. Maybe if you had a bit more to sweeten the deal I could be enticed."

Monos looks in disgust, "You would really ask for more in our time of need?"

Ralph shrugs, "Hahaha yes. Well I see you have nothing so I'm just going to keep watching maybe someone else will have the funds to get my services, well to the air." Ralph takes off watching as Hawkins struggles against the barrier constantly punching against it.

Brainstorm falls to one knee feeling the stress of Hawkins's attacks. Hawkins drives one mighty blow into the barrier shattering it. Brainstorm staggers back from the attack as Hawkins rampages forward delivering a massive fist to his face. Brainstorm's jaw cracks as he rockets off the shore and into the lake with a heavy splash. Hawkins walks forward grabbing the villains under his arm he jumps off and dashes away running into an alleyway. Ralph watches as Hawkins speeds off leaving his view he shrugs before returning to the ground gathering up the rest of the heroes.

"Dang it he got away and he took the bait with him!" Brainstorm says with anger on his face.

Monos holds his side breathing heavily he shakes his head, "We need to get out of here and recover from this…Hawkins will be the next major target; he is too powerful to be left unchecked."

As they get ready to leave a helicopter descends from above landing in front of them the side door opens. General Niesse steps out in his formal attire with his arms behind his back he walks over to the characters with a fierce look on his face.

Brainstorm and Monos step forward to meet him as he stops a short distance from the characters. "General Niesse to what do we owe the pleasure?" Brainstorm asks with curiosity.

Niesse looks at them with rage in his eyes, "You all are nothing but a waste!!! Here it is you have powers and yet all you do is add to the destruction, useless vigilantes! You all are lucky that you are the only small defense that is left against the others. Mark my words though, once we get the aid required I will wipe you all off the face of the earth!"

"Niesse come on, we are trying our best here. They are powerful; you saw what happened last time your soldiers went up against them." Landlord says begrudgingly.

Niesse spits on the ground, "You damn fools think that I care how powerful they are? You all are just as much of a threat every time you clash you destroy something, who pays for that certainly not you idiots. Sure you come by and do a bit to help out but that doesn't change that you are the root cause of it. Mark my words after I'm done with those guys I'm coming after you all. And President Roy isn't going to stop me."

Niesse turns around heading back into the copter he slams the door shut as the propeller begins to spin. The helicopter takes off leaving the dispirited heroes on the ground before zooming off into the distance. The group of five return to their penthouse home watching a recap of the battle on the news after cleaning and addressing their wounds they hold their heads down.

"Hahaha that was a good hit," Ralph says enjoying the broadcast while looking around for more food. "Well I think I did well enough though you didn't catch them completely so I'm still on board till that is done, if it goes on much longer the costs will go up."

Brainstorm shoots an annoyed look at Ralph, "This isn't a game Ralph! People have died and what have we to show for it? Nothing. We haven't stopped the criminals, we haven't saved the world."

Tyreal walks over to the balcony looking out he places his hand on the glass, "Next time we really have to go for it. No more trying to save everyone we will have to kill them."

Monos turns sharply, "That isn't what we do, but we will do more next time definitely."

Tyreal looks back at him, "Well more may not be enough Matthew. Sometimes for the greater good sacrifices must be made. I know you feel responsible for this, and for Katz, you told me all of that before. That doesn't change the fact that he needs to die."

Monos shakes his head, "If we kill him how are we supposed to be any better than they are?"

Tyreal responds, "Sometimes it isn't about being better. Sometimes all that matters is getting the job done. The end justifies the means."

Chapter 6: Fall of the Titans

Katz walks down a road hearing the people talk about the battle and the capture of his team he rolls his eyes while strolling down the dark cold streets of Chicago. He passes by a subway exit seeing three military officers walking up the stairs he slides behind the exit and into a corridor. Katz places his ear as close to the edge as he can as he listens in.

"Niesse said we need to get back to the base guys. We have a shipment from the weapons facility," one of them says.

The second officer jumps clapping his hands, "Haha we'll finally be able to kill those freaks. Let's go."

The three run off jumping into their Humvee they speed away out of the city. Katz squints giving off a low grumbling sound he whips his cape behind him before taking to the air, he hovers steadily with his arms crossed and his eyes closed.

Thinking to himself as he flies, "They stole my people...and now the military has gusto again...this is all your fault Matthew Monos, you and Hawkins. Time to get their attention I say...yes. Attention hmm...that's what I'll do yes."

Katz looks around finding a familiar news icon he rushes over blazing through the air. He bursts through the glass windows and into the newsroom, sliding across the floor he stops directly in front of the camera appearing to the city on the late night news.

The anchors and crew scream in terror running back from Katz as he dusts himself off throwing down the glass from his afro he squints. "Eww when last was the outside of that glass cleaned...oh well I guess." The people watching jump back seeing Katz on the screen they shake their heads.

Back at the penthouse Ralph turns his eyes sharply to the news seeing Katz he smirks, "The last one for my payment...I guess he is back."

Katz turns to the anchors giving them a perturbed look he commands them to sit back down. "Now then I will not have you fools screaming and running about like morons. This isn't the first time that we have broken into this station. You know that Lexi.... Follow the usual drill and everything will be fine. Everyone watches for some odd reason when we attack here. Oops.

"Now then on to more pressing matters, I would like this replayed at least once an hour, more if that suits your fancy. The message is simple, bring me my boys and you will live. That goes out to all of you Monos, Brainstorm, Tyreal, and Landlord. You all know that I am a very capable man, I have been lenient to allow my youngsters to go at it with you, but that does not mean I won't be go off on you guys if you don't return them. So here is the deal, I'm going to blow up this city if you don't return them to me within two days…maybe faster than that if it suits me. After I blow up the entirety of Chicago, I will hunt you down and beat you, each, and every one of you. Until one of you tells me where they are at. I am being generous here, two days is a lot of time, I'll be over the lake…you know where to find me. That is all."

Katz takes off flying through the broken window he turns upwards disappearing behind the clouds as the crew continues to sit there in shock and awe. One of the anchors scrambles for her phone, but she falls from the desk tripping over a wire in her fright as the night passes on.

During the next day Arcos and the others wake up, finding themselves in a large parlor. A short distance from them stands Hawkins in his human form, he pours out a glass of juice before turning around walking over to the group he pulls up a chair.

"Well, well, well looks like the beauties are awake finally took you all long enough." Hawkins says while taking a sip of his juice.

Arcos shakes his head, "Hey now…don't call me a beauty I'm a guy….what happened, and why are you here?"

Hawkins shrugs, "Tisk, tisk that is no way to talk to the man who saved you all from certain capture now is it? Anyway I'm here because I decided it would be good for us to clear the air a little and because you all can lead me to Katz. What happened was you all got beat and you were about to be captured when I came in and took on all of those hero people and saved you from certain incarceration. Does that explain enough for you?"

Sentry nods, "Good enough for now…ugh, I have no intention of leading you to the boss though."

"Hahaha," laughs Hawkins, "As though it matters what you have any intention of doing. You all are free to go at any time, but either way I'll find him by following you or waiting till tomorrow."

Sentry looks up confused, "Why do you say that? What happens tomorrow?"

Hawkins responds, "Katz will reveal himself on the lake. He is expecting you all to be delivered to him unharmed, I would think and if you aren't then he said he was going to blow up the city. You know how Katz is after all."

Titallic gets up stretching his arms he staggers around slightly disoriented. "Well we have to get back to boss then join in on the destruction!"

Arcos squints over to Titallic, "Or we can let him do as he pleases, drawing the attention of those heroes and allowing us to capitalize on it killing them all! Well aside from Katz he will just be a little hurt."

Titallic nods, "Oh yeah…I forgot we aren't playing on his side anymore."

Sentry shakes his head at both of them, "Obviously guys going rogue didn't work out for us. We need the boss."

Arcos rolls his eyes, "Sentry if you want to run back to the boss then do so, but don't expect us to follow along like puppies to their master. I know what I'm doing is right, and if Hawkins wants to find Katz then let him follow along."

Hawkins laughs taking another drink of his juice, "This is grand oh what has Katz done now. I'll tag along and I'll handle Katz, if you all can keep those weaklings off my back."

Sentry gets up heading for the door, "You all just wait boss won't be pleased."

"Wait!" Titallic yells, "Sentry you need to stay if you leave I don't know what Arcos will do with you. You may not make it to the boss."

Sentry turns around with a sharp look in his eyes, "Arcos knows better than that. The agreement was that boss wouldn't be harmed if you can't keep that promise then I'm out!"

Hawkins walks over patting Sentry on the back, "Katz always tells me how loyal you are. Not to worry I don't plan on killing or harming him truthfully all he has to do is say he is sorry. That's all I ask for nothing more. After that we can be good friends again, trust me if I really hated him you all would be dead right now." Sentry squints as he takes a step away from the door.

Back at the military base four massive crates are opened by the soldiers outside. Niesse stands watching the soldiers remove multiple guns and large missiles. Wizencut starts, "Nice aren't they Niesse?"

Niesse turns looking over at Wizencut he nods. "Yes but what are these presents?"

Wizencut responds, "The latest experimental weaponry from Cadmus Research Facility. They only have these so try not to waste them all the new laser rifles should be able to pierce their skin unlike the bullets. And a missile is to go on one of the jets that arrived today; it is powered by some of the same technology that we were trying to obtain from Katz those years back. When used it will create a small dimensional fissure where a fusion reaction will occur. Try not to fire the missiles in the city at all costs. The reaction has only been tested a few times who knows how powerful it really is or what sort of chain reaction it could cause when it is launched."

Niesse smiles, "Finally a fighting chance against those freaks. We will use them all tomorrow, we already know exactly where Katz will be but I'll have the men on alert today just in case they try anything."

Wizencut responds, "Good enough I suppose the rest of this mission is in your hands Niesse, I have other things to attend to for now, oh and President Roy said that this is it after this you pull out and we only do recovery efforts, his points are down and all. This warring in the country isn't looking good for him so you better pull it off."

Niesse spits on the ground again, "I don't give a damn about his points all I care about is finally getting rid of those creatures and avenge my brother."

Wizencut laughs, "Oh you Niesse you keep it up and you might just have a heart attack before you see them dead. Regardless I shall depart from this you can have it. We will be monitoring your progress from Washington." Wizencut gives Niesse a salute before walking off heading back inside.

As the day passes Katz remains in the air looking down over the lake and the city seeing nothing. As the light begins to wane Brainstorm flies up floating behind Katz. He turns to Brainstorm staring at him with uncaring eyes Brainstorm nods, "Katz it's been a while since I've seen you in person."

Katz slowly blinks before releasing a sigh, "That it has Brainstorm and your point is…?"

Brainstorm continues, "We don't have to do this tomorrow just come with me and we can work something out. As far as your people go Hawkins took them on his own we didn't want him too and we tried to stop him."

Katz sighs, "Don't you think I know that already? What I said on the air the other night was just to try to get him riled up but I should have known Hawkins would be too smart for that. Blasted man oh well."

Brainstorm looks on hopeful, "So you aren't going to destroy the city?"

Katz's eyes quickly shift to a squint as he stares at Brainstorm, "You think I lied about everything? I can assure you this won't be like the last time. I will ruin you and everyone else that gets in my way. Arcos and the others may have been right I have been too soft and now look what happened. Time to show this world who is really in charge I've played with you all enough. This is the last time you get a pass come tomorrow if you try to stop me I will run you through."

Brainstorm shakes his head, "That's all I needed to know. I'll see you tomorrow."

He flies off reporting his finds to Monos, "I was reading his mind the entire time he is planning to launch the attack tomorrow night at around 7 pm. I think that means we need to get there early like at 3 in the morning."

Monos nods, "Yeah he probably knows you would read his mind and gave you a false time. Or does he know that you would read the false time and predict something earlier….anyway I'm going to get suited up and ready. This isn't going to end well I think." The heroes prepare themselves leaving within a few hours they fly with Ralph towards the lake.

Shadows creep across the land while Katz floats, the breeze whipping his cape around. From above Albert drops down hovering next to Katz he gives him a look. "Katz what are you doing? They played your message all day yesterday President Roy even made a statement about bringing this all to an end. Are you ready for whatever it is they have planned?"

Katz shrugs, "I doubt they can do anything really. But if not I will do as I said and destroy this city, really this region. Albert I warn you now when the time comes you better fly upward and fly fast. The amount of power I'll be putting out will be disgusting."

Albert says, "Are you sure about that, I can see it on your face you don't really want to do you?"

Katz closes his eyes thinking, "Well no not really, but I must stand by what I have said. We can't have these people constantly thinking they can stand up to me. This city will be a shining example for the rest to follow suit."

Katz turns his sight to the city of Chicago watching the gleaming lights in the distance sparkle off the water in front of him his hands fall to his side as he takes a deep breath. "Well Albert it will soon be time, I think they will show up shortly, and with any luck Hawkins will be bringing Sentry and the others. Please prepare the atmosphere for this."

Albert nods, "You got it Katz," closing his eyes he focuses his mind and body, constantly releasing an aura of energy.

His short blond hair whips around as the wind begins to pick up and a dense fog begins to seep over the city from the water. The fog sways in and out of the streets covering a large area of the city as large black clouds rumble overhead. Lightning sparks from cloud to cloud jumping sporadically, as more bolts crash down on the water's surface. The wind grows strong whistling through the columns of downtown Chicago, as the people remaining outside quickly move for shelter. Small pelts of rain fall from the sky crashing into the streets and buildings below as Brainstorm and the others can be seen in the distance.

Albert opens his eyes yawning he turns to Katz. "Well what is the plan?"

"I'll handle this you just provide back up. Your main objective should be to keep Brainstorm busy; I'd rather not have him mucking around in my head while I'm annihilating the rest of his team." Katz says while stretching his arms.

Albert scratches the back of his head, "You know sometimes I think you are a little bit bipolar or something…just thought I'd let you know that."

Katz squints, "Yeah probably, but it works for now we can deal with that after I'm done with this.

Seconds later the group of heroes and Ralph stop in front of Katz and Albert feeling the heavier rain drops Monos floats forward. "Katz, Albert stand down now and surrender we know exactly what you are plotting and we will not allow it to happen."

Katz rolls his eyes, "What has it been a year since we parted and yet your lines are still lame. Mine too probably but I digress. Matthew Monos and crew tonight is the end."

Brainstorm interjects, "Katz it doesn't have to be like this! Listen to reason!"

Katz responds lightly, "Oh but it does, Albert ready? Let's blitz."

The heroes quickly take up a defensive stance as Katz clenches his fists exploding around him is an aura of atomic energy. Katz takes his right hand extending from his side he points out with two fingers. Katz then slides the fingers down through the air cutting apart the dimensional fabric. Ralph raises an eyebrow in shock, Katz reaches through into a different dimension and pulls his hand out with a sword in his palm. The curved metal blade shines in the darkness while the circular hilt rests on top of Katz's fingers.

"Haha you know I do enjoy my swordplay," Katz says before speeding through the air heading directly for Monos.

Tyreal steps up spreading his cape behind him he launches an array of chains towards Katz, but he dodges around the chains with ease moving at blinding speeds he appears in front of Tyreal slashing upwards he cuts through Tyreal's suit with his sword breaking the blade in the process.

Katz squints again in annoyance, "Blasted human made weapons just aren't made to be swung with such force…."

Tyreal slides back holding the wound he releases some of his energy into his suit healing himself and repairing the damage to his costume. Katz throws the broken sword down to the water below as Tyreal, Ralph, and Landlord dash at him from three directions. Katz lifts his knee blocking Tyreal; he then raises both arms stopping a punch from both Landlord and Ralph. With all of his strength Katz releases a pulse of atomic energy blowing the three characters away.

He sprints through the air throwing multiple punches at Landlord with ferocious speed. Landlord is struck by a number of blows, but he slowly catches on countering the attacks with his own fists. Katz drops down dodging a straight from Landlord; he rises up grabbing onto Landlord's arm he flips Landlord throwing him down to the water below.

Tyreal rises above Katz blasting down at him with an array of chain spears. Katz turns quickly seeing the attack he opens a dimensional tear behind him as he descends quickly slipping through the portal he avoids the sharp spears vanishing from view. Lightning strikes around the characters as they search for Katz.

Brainstorm's eyes turn purple as he begins to sense for Katz when suddenly Albert charges him tackling Brainstorm. He grabs his arm and tosses him into the fog covered shore. Brainstorm gets up sliding through the sand, he looks up to see a bolt of lightning coming down towards him. Brainstorm pulls up one hand lifting the water from the lake before him he deflects the electricity. Albert breaks through the water with a flying kick. Brainstorm sees the attack stepping to the side he watches as Albert smashes into the sand with a massive plume of dust.

Brainstorm then waves his hands forward releasing a psychic wave across the shoreline blowing Albert out of the sand and onto the road.

Katz appears through another portal slamming his elbow into Tyreal's back, he grabs the staggered hero by the head. His hand begins to glow with atomic energy when suddenly Ralph pulls Katz down with his gravity force dropping Katz under the lake he forces Katz down to the bottom holding him there.

Katz staggers trying to get up under the heavy force he opens another tear under him falling through he drops down on top of Ralph. Katz kicks off from Ralph, he extends one arm as his eyes gleam with energy. He fires off an atomic beam down at Ralph. The blast slams into Ralph's chest forcing him into the water it explodes sending water flowing over the shores and splashing high into the rain filled air. Katz smirks when from behind Landlord grapples him in a bear hug.

Monos floats in front of Katz shaking his head, "This has to stop."

Katz laughs, "And you think this will work. I see you are still just as passive as ever, you won't last much longer."

Monos shakes his head once more in depression, "I didn't want to have to do this but here goes."

He attempts to use his powers again as he reaches into Katz's emotions, but Katz elbows Landlord's stomach breaking free of his grip, he grabs Landlord by the hand and tosses him at Monos. The two spiral out of the air completely out of control as Katz builds up energy in both of his palms.

Tyreal speeds in wrapping Katz up in his chains he spins him quickly. Tyreal then flies in striking Katz with an uppercut he sends the villain flying higher into the lightning storm. Tyreal gives chase catching up with his foe he spins towards him with a strong kick. Katz barely blocks the attack being pushed across the clouds as a lightning bolt passes between the two characters. Katz regains his focus, seeing Tyreal blitzing toward him he fires off three atomic beams, but Tyreal dodges around each of them. Katz then charges back as the two clash a loud clap of thunder rumbles from the skies above.

Tyreal blocks a punch from Katz grabbing his fist in his open palm he pulls Katz forward striking his gut with a strong knee. Tyreal then lifts his hands above Katz clasping them together like a hammer he brings them down in an attempt to strike Katz in the back. Katz moves quickly pushing off of Tyreal's knee he knocks him in the face with his back. Katz then follows through with a swift elbow to the side of Tyreal's face knocking him from the sky.

Katz speeds after Tyreal zigzagging through the air he tackles Tyreal and accelerates crashing into the ground with a massive impact. Ralph crawls from the water bleeding and hurt he struggles to his feet while Monos and Landlord pick themselves up gathering around the shore.

An explosion appears on the road as Brainstorm is tossed through the air the metal pipes under the ground are pulled up floating in the air Albert throws them at Brainstorm but he blocks with a psychic barrier flipping over he lands on the beach as Albert jumps down appearing next to Katz.

"This isn't going well Katz." Albert says with a heavy breath.

Katz nods, "Hahaha, we are outnumbered I will say that. But this is hardly over. The winds of change are on the way…at least I hope."

Landlord, Tyreal, and Brainstorm prepare to attack as Katz and Albert give each other a high five and dash off into the air. A massive wall of earth rises from the sand chasing after Albert as he flies into the city from the left. Brainstorm snaps his fingers calling down a tornado he flies into the center of it raining down psychic bolts at Katz while Tyreal flies after Katz firing green energy blasts. Katz sways around spinning and spiraling he takes the fight into the city as he twirls around the corners of the buildings dodging the attacks.

Katz turns around while flying away he fires off two atomic beams before turning around and accelerating away, he flies upward along the side of the Willis tower. The two atomic blasts explode blowing away the tornado and knocking Brainstorm into a building while Tyreal falls down sliding through the road he crashes into the front of a bus.

Albert turns rushing over the water as the earth turns into a snake gliding over the pond it chases after him. A cyclone rises behind Albert shooting through the head of the earth snake shattering the attack.

Ralph gets up preparing to chase after Albert he jumps into the air when suddenly a blast of electricity surges through his body dropping him to the ground instantly. Monos turns behind him to see Sentry, Arcos and Titallic appearing from the fog. Sentry steps forward, "You aren't killing our boss!"

Arcos laughs, "That's our job…to beat him up at least." Sentry squints at Arcos before running off towards the city trailing after Katz.

Monos quickly jumps back to a defensive stance shaking his head, "Dang…I wasn't expecting that…"

Katz lands on the ground breathing heavily he rubs his forehead before walking down the road finding Tyreal with his head stuck in a bus. "Well looks like things just aren't going your way this morning. I think you will be the first to die."

Katz covers his left hand in an atomic energy blade raising it up to slice off Tyreal's head he swings it down when a car sails through the air slamming into Katz's chest he crashes into a pillar. Hawkins grabs Tyreal by the back pulling him from the bus he smashes his fist into Tyreal's chest launching him high and out into the lake. Katz pushes the car to the side wiping the blood from his lip he stares in a daze seeing his long-time rival he shakes his head. Hawkins stands over him grabbing him around the waist with one hand he lifts Katz up to his face while pushing up his glasses.

"Well...Dr. K.S. Katz how long has it been?" Hawkins says with a pompous tone.

Katz shakes his head yawning he rolls his eyes, "Dang it J.! Did you have to throw a car at me?! Like really! That hurt ugh you have gotten stronger."

Hawkins spouts one word, "Katz."

"Hawkins," Katz says in an arrogant tone matching Hawkins. The two stare at each other as Hawkins releases Katz a moment later.

"I'll take that for now," Hawkins says turning away he begins to walk towards the shore.

Katz chases after him catching up the two stroll down the road, "Wait a minute you will accept that no, no, no. Listen here Hawkins you got in my way and ruined my plan! Now where are my boys?"

Hawkins laughs, "Oh Katz fool. Those pesky children wouldn't go along with my plan at all. I tried but Arcos specifically is interested in taking control from you. Sentry is loyal to a tee though."

Katz rolls his eyes, "Well of course they are like that. I already know that we need to hurry up though I can finally end those heroes all at once."

Hawkins grumbles, "You won't do that, they will defeat you without my help that is, and you aren't getting anything until you apologize and give me $50."

Katz's jaw drops as he stares up at Hawkins, "You best believe you aren't getting either of those!" The two continue forward but they stop a short distance from the battle at the shore. Numerous soldiers appear through the fog lined up in front of them with guns locked and ready.

Katz rolls his eyes taking a few steps ahead of Hawkins, "I got this watch a pro at work old man. Listen up soldiers you will die this morning so please say your piece that I may end you on a proper note."

The soldiers sit in silence when suddenly laser fire speeds through the fog towards Katz. Katz cocks his eyebrow up as the lasers bounce off his metal armor plate, "What are you all…"

A second shot hits him in the shoulder as blood splatters across the ground. Katz staggers back falling to one knee he grabs his shoulder as another blast hits him in the leg and another on the arm. Hawkins quickly jumps high avoiding the blasts as he climbs the sides of the buildings while Katz ignites the ground blasting a wall of atomic energy forward he disintegrates the soldiers.

Sentry, seeing the attack, lands next to Katz seeing the wounds he helps him up, "Boss what happened?"

Katz mumbles, "Ahh…that really hurt, oww. The military has a new weapon…dang…give me a minute."

The sound of laser fire comes through the distance as Katz looks forward shaking his head, "Never mind then let's get back to the shore we need to save the others." A flash of atomic energy runs over Katz rebuilding the atomic bonds and regenerating his wounds.

Sentry and Katz fly off as Hawkins follows them. At the shore a platoon of military soldiers stand raining down laser fire on the heroes and the villains, while General Niesse sits in his helicopter watching. The roar of jets comes from above while the character step back towards the water.

Arcos snaps his fingers but the guns continue to fire. "Damn it, they aren't electronic guns how is that possible!"

Titallic stands in front of Arcos deflecting the lasers with his metal skin he looks around for the end of the troop lines. Electricity jumps around his fingers as he takes aim when a tank shell smashes into his chest pushing him into the water and knocking Arcos over. A number of soldiers appear around Arcos firing off their laser blasts Arcos tries to cover himself. He turns towards the attack a few seconds later feeling nothing he looks up to see Katz before him. A large dimensional tear absorbs the shots as multiple tears behind the soldiers mow them down.

Katz extends his hand out to Arcos helping him to his feet. "Katz…I mean boss…you are here."

Katz nods, "As I said silly youth, so impatient you didn't think I didn't see you plotting against me forever and a day ago. I still wasn't going to leave you to die...though I should it might teach you a lesson...then again...if you are dead is it really a lesson at all?"

Arcos nods while Titallic pulls himself from the water. "Now then there is no time to discuss your punishments for now you all just defend me from these army fools and those so called heroes, I'll handle the rest." Katz says as he spirals into the air flying quickly he stops near the center of the lake.

A jet passes by heading directly after Katz it fires its chain gun. The bullets slam into Katz nearly knocking him from the air he barely regains his balance as he squints shaking his fist.

Katz then rises above the water stopping, he spreads his arms out holding his position steady he begins to create a massive dimensional tear behind him. The waters below begin to churn and spin as the air grows heavy as another tear in the dimensions appears in the distance. Katz's eyes turn dark as he expels more energy creating more tears. Several more jets rocket through the air bombarding the characters with missiles.

Three missiles smash into Hawkins knocking him down to one knee and then into the lake. More missiles cross through the air as Albert takes the missiles deflecting them with ease he sends them back destroying three of the planes. Several missiles head towards Katz but Albert flies over quickly crushing three of them. Another one passes by Albert rushing for Katz as more tears appear around the city causing the earth to shake and the air to crackle. Arcos forces the missile to short circuit dropping it in the water below as Sentry and Titallic join up around Katz.

Bolts of energy begin to surge through the tears as Brainstorm runs over to Monos, "What's going on Monos? This isn't good..."

Matt looks around seeing Katz in the distance he nods to the remaining heroes as they fly off heading towards Katz. "Guys we need to stop him now...the amount of power that Katz is putting out will only destroy everything. Brainstorm analyzes his mind find out what he is doing."

Brainstorm reaches in to Katz's mind only getting a fraction of his thoughts. He looks over at the others. "Monos we need to stop him now! This technique is his most powerful attack. It will destroy the entire region if we don't end it within the next minute!"

Brainstorm looks to the skies calling down lightning bolts towards Katz as the lightning rains down Titallic fires off electricity countering the bolts. Ralph tries to pull the entire group down constantly increasing the gravity around them but Albert tosses three more jets at him. The jets open fire under Arcos's command blasting the heroes out of the sky with their missiles.

Several jets dash downward appearing above they catch the villains off guard as several missiles crash into the group. A single jet flies forward firing the fusion missile at the vulnerable Katz it slams into his chest creating a massive explosion in the skies above Lake Michigan. Katz is forced back flying into the tear he vanishes. The other portals crackle and fade as the central vortex expands pulling in the other characters one by one they all sink into the main portal before it closes rippling across the atmosphere, the skies become clear and the water becomes calm. Niesse sits in his helicopter looking out over the lake he scans the area for life finding nothing.

He then picks up his phone calling Wizencut. "Well, Wizencut you can tell President Roy that we have finally freed ourselves from those damn freaks. We lost a lot of good men and the city was damaged again but we are rid of them forever I think. I'll be back in Washington in a few days for my reward." Niesse grins while hanging up the phone.

Arc II: ENTER THE DRAGON
Chapter 7: Revisit

Sentry gets up holding his head in pain he barely moves while looking around. The sky glistens with a heavy red light as black lightning strikes in the distance. He moves his hand through the red dry dirt, he pulls himself to his knees feeling heavy and sluggish; Sentry continues to gaze around. A short distance away he sees a tattered cape waving in the light wind. Katz stands at the side of the cliff looking out over the field his eyes quiver as his lip trembles. A heavy sense of fear looms over his head, as he continues to gaze out on the land in shock.

"...ugh grr... I... didn't think... no... not again... never again...no." Katz's armor falls to the ground cracked and ruined by the missile he slumps down to his knees shaking his head.

The others slowly rise waking from their crash landing they struggle to their feet like Sentry while Albert stumbles over to Katz looking out over the cliff he scratches his head before his eyes grow wide, "Katz...we can't be here."

Katz looks up to Albert with great despair, "I have to get out of here...we need to get out of here...we can't be here of all places."

Albert nods helping Katz to his feet he turns to see the heroes rising and Hawkins back in his human form. The other villains begin to gather around while Arcos attempts to fly but he fails falling on the ground. "Now Katz you're going to have to do something about them as well. You know they won't understand what has happened. We will need you to lead us out of this place."

Katz rests one of his hands over his forehead looking down at the ground below the cliff, his head pounding with fear and pain. "This is the last thing I wanted. Alas you are right." Straightening himself, Katz picks up his shattered armor throwing it off the side of the cliff while Monos and the other stare around in dismay.

Katz turns to the group looking them over he takes up his courage, "Alright boys you all are in for quite a shocker."

Arcos steps forward, "Boss...umm...where are we and why can't I fly?"

"I can't read or feel anyone's minds myself... and I'm getting hungry." Brainstorm interjects.

"I'm so heavy...and kind of tired," says Sentry.

Katz shakes his head, "You all be silent I will explain but first we need to get moving off this cliff and towards those pillars over there."

Katz points to his right as the group turns and looks they see in the far distance several large towers circling around another more massive structure. From the central tower a beam of red light rises upward and into the atmosphere passing behind the clouds.

"That is where we will be going...this friends is where I was after that explosion at my lab. I spent a year here...or so they say in the real world. Welcome to what I would say is the den of Satan, but I'm sure that is far worse than here. As far as your powers and abilities go, the majority of them won't work here. As long as that tower remains active that is. It fills the air with some sort of neutralizer. The strength of the poison depends on the strength of the person and how long you inhale it. To be honest you all if I can take an educated guess, you should still retain your strength and durability for now. Though after a while that too will even begin to wane until you are basically human again."

They steadily rise bandaging their wounds with their capes and whatever cloth they can find before heading off. Katz walks pass the group; looking out he sees a small jagged path down the side of the cliff that opens into a long smooth slope. He slides down the path followed by the others while Arcos squints taking up the rear between the villains and the heroes.

As they make it down to the larger slope they see a large dense open area before them and a short ways away a lush forest of black and grey trees. Near the edge of the forest rests a steel like structure long and wide it sits on the tip of the barren waste.

"So boss what else can you tell me about this place and how did we end up here?" Sentry asks as he skips forward walking along side Katz and Albert.

Katz looks at him, "Well the most important thing is that we get into that building down there before the darkness comes. If I remember correctly and if time is at least somewhat what it was when I first got here we should have about six hours before nightfall if you want to call it that. If we are out after then we better be ready there are creatures out here that prowl around and enjoy meat if you get my drift. As far as how we ended up here well... I'm not exactly sure, though I can assume. Whatever was in that last missile was something new. The strangest thing is that it seemed to be based off of my research, the energy output was way higher than the usual military yields. So basically they reproduced my experiment…I honestly don't know how everyone else got dragged into the portal, but I suppose that doesn't really matter now that we are all here anyway. I'll come up with some countermeasures for the next time; but for now I guess I'll just not use that technique ever again."

Monos and Brainstorm step up, "Katz and your lackeys since you have no powers we suggest that you surrender."

Katz, Albert and Sentry slowly turn their heads back to Monos and Brainstorm each of them looking greatly confused and annoyed they stare at the two heroes. "What, are you serious right now…really…Monos, Brainstorm you two are a piece of work. You have no powers by which to speak of and I'm your only guide through this area, not to mention the only one who has ever returned from this dimension and you have the nerve to say such stupid things…." Katz says with the most disgusted look on his face.

He then turns back ahead jumping down a set of stones he lands on the open plain looking out on the cracked dry ground with small bushes and grass growing in patches. Brainstorm and Monos slide to the back, after being told off, they walk quietly. The group slowly begins to cross the large open field with Katz in the lead. They look around constantly searching for shadows and creatures. High above the group the lightning bolts continue to ripple across the clouds blocking out most of the light.

"So umm boss, I guess you aren't really mad about that whole mutiny and taking over thing right?" Arcos asks with a small voice.

Katz continues to walk on for a few seconds before responding, "I was never mad per say. It takes effort to get me mad. I can easily be disappointed and sometimes even upset but not mad. No. Rather though you will be broken of this rebellious attitude the moment that we get back know that."

Arcos looks down with a twinge of fear in his eyes, "Yes boss."

Ralph walks on with his face down, looking completely distraught while Landlord walks next to him. "What's the matter Ralph?"

Ralph continues on staring down he mutters, "All of the money that you guys owe me. If we don't get back, I won't get it. Dude you have no idea how upset I am right now. It is like I was working for free or for the good of people or some crap. Like really."

"You're upset about money…." Landlord says with an outraged stare on his face, "We could have died from that attack and you are worried about money…."

"Hahaha, you two should probably take a break from each other. Besides from what Monos told me, Katz is an expert at getting out of things like this." Tyreal says jumping in between the two. "Anyway I was wondering bout that. How did we survive those missiles and what were they packing? I've been hit with attacks like that before, but that was different."

Landlord nods, "Yeah I think it was some new energy thing. I hope they don't use it on us again. We need to get them to see us as friends and allies rather than enemies."

Tyreal agrees, "Yeah if we bring these guys in when we get back then we should be seen for the heroes that we are."

"If you all survive this you won't have the energy to survive us," Titallic says sharply eyeing the three characters. "Don't think for a second that we are buddy, buddy just because the majority of my powers are gone."

Albert shakes his head listening to the banter in the back. "Katz I will never understand how you fell in with this crowd of people. What a rambunctious bunch…."

Katz responds, "Well you know how the story goes we will deal with them all when time comes."

The ground beneath them begins to shake steadily with a slow rumble as cracks appear along the sides of their path. Along the right side geysers of fire race upward and into the clouds dissipating them as they burn into the atmosphere. The group jumps back staring at the fire while Katz raises an eyebrow in confusion.

He looks over to see the facility building a short distance away before turning back to the others. "Get moving now. Nightfall is imminent and we can't be out here."

"But you said we had hours!!!" barks Tyreal as he scrambles forward.

Katz squints, "Yeah and now I'm telling you to move so shut up and move fool. Or get eaten by the creatures."

The characters begin to charge forward tired and drained they drag their bodies across the barren plains nearing the facility as the clouds begin to part revealing the soft and weak light of several large moons. A strange unfamiliar scream is heard in the distance followed by the patter of feet on the ground as more flames race upwards from the fields behind them.

On top of the cliff where they landed heavy black claws crash down on the ground scraping around as a long snout sniffs the area. A screaming purr echoes off the cliff as four long slick legs clank and slam across the ground heading down the slope and on to the field. Sentry arrives at the facility first looking around the building in the darkness he feels across its smooth metal surface looking for an entrance. As Katz arrives he stops on the side of the building panting he looks back. The others come barreling over stopping at the building as well they each look around wondering what to do next.

"Well Katz stop wasting your time gathering breath and open the damn door!" screams Hawkins as he stands over Katz looking down in annoyance.

Katz shoots a glare back at Hawkins with his cheeks puffed up, "Hey now old man you listen here! If I need to catch my breath then I need to catch my breath! Besides I haven't been inside of this building before! I have no clue how to get in, how would you like it if I said that and meant it! Now shut up and let me think."

Katz rests his fingers on his forehead tapping away at his skull he closes his eyes while feeling around the walls of the building. Katz continues walking as the clopping sound gets closer.

Suddenly a door opens sliding upward the light from the inside of the building shines outward. The characters quickly run into the building as the door closes down fiercely behind them. Just outside the walls of the building a heavy thud is heard followed by a number of crashes against the wall and strange howls just outside the door. Katz slides down against the door, breathing a sigh of relief while the others look around checking out the large facility. The walls are covered in shimmering heated metal warming the rooms while the floors are smooth with carpet. As the group strolls through corridors they find a large open cafeteria area with round tables and large strange ovens. Hawkins opens a closet to find stores of bread. He pulls the bread out noticing that it is fresh.

"Guys someone must have been here recently. This isn't old and moldy at all." Hawkins says while examining the bread.

"I also found some sort of meat over here!" yells Tyreal, "I don't know if it's kosher but it looks good. We have a meal!" The others gather around slowly figuring how to work the kitchen area they begin to cook meat and prepare the bread. Sentry and Titallic come in with other random food bits while Katz shakes his head walking down the hallway.

Katz swings down a corner and into a corridor with multiple rooms. "Ahh this must be the bedrooms or whatever they would be called."

"Now Katz why aren't you joining the others?" Albert says while walking up alongside him.

Katz bobs his head around, "Well I figured it best to do a bit of exploring. This building is close in structure to one that I already stayed in but it is larger. Besides you never know what you will find in these places."

Albert nods, "Yeah that is right I guess we do need to know more about the area. I don't even know what to tell Emily when we get back. We have to hurry."

Katz responds, "I know but without our abilities we can't do much at all. To be honest with you though, I turned off that tower last time I was here. I in fact rerouted that power to create the wormhole to get back home but somehow it is back on and I don't understand it at all."

Albert opens one of the doors looking inside the room he sees a large capsule tube in the center glistening metal walls are covered with numerous images of some strange humanoid creatures.

Walking over Albert places his hand over one of the pictures before turning back looking at Katz, "So what do you think happened to them? They seem to be human like at least from what I can see in these pictures."

Katz sighs, "I'm sure they were very close to what we are now, though I don't know how they got here and what happened to them. They were definitely more advance, those creatures outside are stopped by a force field if it wasn't for that, they would have already ran through the metal exterior and came upon us."

As the two continue down the hallway a thought comes to Albert, "Wait a minute if you turned it off when you were leaving how do you know that is what is inhibiting our abilities?

Katz shrugs, "I don't, but it sounded good at the time so I used it. They needed a good enough motivation to get them moving towards the tower. I figured why just give them one when they can have two."

Albert ponders asking, "What do you want done with those hero types? You know they won't rest unless we surrender and when we get back it will start again."

Katz rolls his eyes as the two head up a flight of stairs and down another pathway. "To be fair I'm actually hoping that while they are here they can finally get over this justice crap and come to the proper side." And if not at least allow us to do as we please and go stop some regular criminals. Knowing them though they will persist and then I will have to kill them though I would rather not."

Albert shakes his head, "You are still too soft Katz, always have been and always will be. You know eventually everyone will see through that tough exterior of yours."

Katz finds a door with a strange keypad on it. He bends down looking at the pad before dashing his fingers across it putting in a random code. The door opens as his eyes grow wide before him stands a large armory. "Albert look at this!"

Albert steps into the armory with Katz along the wall they see numerous vests of alien metal and an assortment of rifle like weaponry. Katz continues on walking over to a wall of various blades and swords he grins.

"Oh goodness you have found swords." Albert says while picking up one of the rifles. He tosses it around feeling the light weight metal as he runs down the long barrel and looks over the sleek design.

Katz pulls down one of the swords looking at the curved glowing metal blade he runs his fingers along the side of the weapon. "Albert you know I'm a swordsman at heart, not really trained very well, but I can swing one pretty fast and quite accurately. I'll just grab a couple of these, new armor, and some new boots while I'm at it."

The armor slides over Katz's shirt as plates extend out from the breastplate they wrap around Katz's back fitting tightly and firm. The silver metal shines in the room as Katz stretches taking breaths in between his movements. He straps two swords along his sides and two more on his back.

Albert laughs while grabbing his own plate of armor along with a rifle and a pistol. The two head back downstairs entering the cafeteria they find the two groups eating at their own tables separated by the vast room between them. Katz looks over to Albert, shrugging, he walks pass Monos and the heroes and over to Hawkins and the rest of his team showing them the weapons and armor to them. "Wow! Boss where did you find all of that...are two of those swords for me?" asks Sentry.

Katz squints, "No. I don't share my swords...you can get your own upstairs."

"Instead of wasting time finding weapons shouldn't you be looking for medical supplies and the like Katz?" Hawkins interjects, "I mean look at us we are bandaged with the tattered rags you use to have swinging behind your body."

Katz stares with his jaw dropped, "How dare you Hawkins. My cape was not at all a rag it was of high value."

Hawkins laughs, "Oh really and how much did it cost you?"

"It was free a gift…." Katz says while taking a seat at the table cracking his knuckles.

Hawkins scoffs, "Free means cheap which means it wasn't worth a damn in the first place, tattered rags it is." With the snap of his fingers Hawkins points at Katz with a grin on his face.

Katz stares and gives off a low grumbling sound as he grabs a piece of bread and begins to chew on it. "Grr…stupid….Hawkins…that's why you will never see that fifty dollar bill ever."

The heroes sit back watching in the distance as they eat in peace. Monos glances back at his team and then over to Katz and the others. "Guys I've come to a decision. We are going to have to put aside our work to capture them while we are here, and try to be cordial."

Tyreal jumps back, "Cordial…you mean nice to them? Why would we do that? They are the ones that caused all of this in the first place. As far as I'm concerned I think we have been too nice to them and that is the problem. We need to force them to surrender or end them, it won't get any better if we are nice to them or not."

Monos nods, "I know and I understand how you feel but still. We are all stuck here together and if we don't work together we won't get out. The only one who has been here before and knows how to get out is Katz. And he is being nice enough to take us along even though he could have left us there on the cliff and went off on his own."

Landlord looks over staring at the villains as he chews on a piece of meat. "The only reason he is being nice is because of you and Brainstorm, if you two weren't here he would have left the rest of us to rot. We should be lucky that you all are old team mates."

Ralph kicks his feet up on the table yawning, "Really I don't care at the moment what you dudes do. I'm gonna eat this here bit of food and I'm gone to bed. You all aren't paying me now so I don't care if you live or die. Who knows if Katz comes upon something valuable I may just be switching sides. And from the looks of those weapons I might say he has."

Ralph finishes his last piece of bread burping loud he kicks off from the table and walks out of the room heading down the long corridor of rooms. He stares at the capsule completely confused while the others finish up their dinner.

Katz walks down the hallway carrying his bread with him while the others slowly head to their own rooms. Katz walks over helping each of them into the capsule and setting it for rest mode.

He stops at Monos's capsule. "Hey umm Katz I just wanted to say thanks for taking us along, I know you didn't have too but I'm glad you did as are the others. They just don't want to admit it."

Katz slides his head up from behind the capsule squinting at Monos, "That's wonderful for you. In actuality though I did have to bring you fools along because I'm sure you would have followed anyway. It isn't like I have my abilities by which I could ditch you all here but the thought has crossed my mind."

Monos laughs, "You know you don't have to pretend to be that way all the time." A low growl comes from Katz as he slides back over to the control panel for the capsule. "Come on Katz I'm serious. You still could have ditched us while we were all wounded or so but you stayed to help get us on our feet. I have already told my friends to be cordial with you all for the duration of this trip, we are going to have to work together to get out of here in one piece."

"If you so say so," says Katz, "Just go to sleep and be ready in the morning. These capsules come with a lot of features I set them on medical sleep mode so you all should be good as new by tomorrow or whenever it is that we get up...I forgot how to get the timer exactly right...haha. We will discuss whenever it is that you all get up." Katz pushes a button closing the capsule as he heads out of the room and back to his own.

Chapter 8: Origins

Titallic's capsule opens slowly as his eyes flutter awake. He slowly rises from the pad, feeling completely rejuvenated, he moves out of the capsule and into the room. He stretches his arms yawning before walking out of the main room and into the bathroom. Moments later he steps out into the hallway to hear voices from further down near the cafeteria. As he walks down to the cafeteria he finds Landlord and Sentry sitting down having a discussion. "Sentry morning, what's he doing here?" Titallic says as he pulls up a chair.

Sentry looks over to Titallic with a smirk, "Hey about time you got up; we almost thought you were dead in there. As for Landlord here we were just about to discuss how it is that we came about our abilities. You want to join in on the conversation?"

Titallic raises an eyebrow, "Why would I want to talk to that guy? He's the enemy last time I checked yep."

Sentry responds, "Well the last time you checked was two days ago…we had a whole day of bonding being that it was just a few of us that got up the first day. Katz and Albert have been out and about while Hawkins has been busy upstairs in the control room for this place. So it has just been me with Landlord, Monos, and Ralph. Ralph isn't much of a conversationalist…as far as I'm concerned."

"You can join us it would be cool to learn more about all of you guys," Landlord says.

Titallic scratches the back of his head, looking over at Sentry. "You've gone soft but I'll bite this time."

Landlord nods, "I'll go first if that is alright with you guys. My real name is Greg, but Landlord works because of my powers of course. It all started about two years ago, and to be honest I'm not really sure how I first gained my abilities they just kind of happened. I was out in Africa on a study abroad trip. I was working on my masters in Agricultural science and economics, which is why I was there, studying just how they used agriculture in their everyday life. Well I was walking through a crop field examining the plants when I feel through a sink hole.

"I landed in a cave far underground; it was quite unusual for that area and all I can remember is looking up and seeing the light in the distance. My body ached horribly and when I reached down to the ground some strange force swept through me, it caused the earth to rumble and rise pushing me from the cavern floor up to the surface. Shortly after that more abilities began to form and I could feel my body getting stronger. I couldn't really control it at first but that was when I ran into Monos and Brainstorm, they helped me get to where I am today."

"Which isn't very far," Titallic says with a snicker.

Landlord looks over with a shocked face, "That's not nice, I'm sharing my life with you guys."

"Come now Titallic let's not spoil everything for Landlord you know he is weak in both mind and body and boss might be upset if we break him already." Sentry says while waving his hand at Titallic.

"Hey!!" yells Landlord.

"J/k Landlord gosh how gullible are you…" Sentry says while squinting, "Titallic you go."

Titallic rolls his eyes slinging his fingers through his black hair he kicks back in the chair. "Well thank you Sentry, the name is Kevin Doppler and I will say this. Like you I just know when my powers first appeared. I was out heading to work at the sub shop in town. I was running late and I went down a back alley to cut some time. That was the wrong idea though, there was a guy with a gun, he held me up and wanted everything I had. I didn't have much so I threw what I had at him but he wasn't done yet.

"I had seen his face and he wasn't going to allow that to slide. He shot me…in the head. But when the bullet hit me it just crumbled and fell to the ground. The guy was shaking and terrified when he ran off I looked down at my hands and they were metal…everything was metal. Electricity was jumping around my body as well, it was so strange. That was about 2 years ago and I haven't looked back since."

"Haha intense, far more intense than what happened to me." Landlord says with excitement.

Titallic shrugs, "Yeah whatever, it wasn't that great when I thought I was about to die."

Landlord responds, "Yeah I guess that would be true. Interesting that you and I both only remember when our powers were first used not when we got them."

Titallic responds, "Yeah well to be honest none of us remember how we got them aside from boss supposedly."

"Yeah, yeah guys. Now onto me," interjects Sentry. Landlord bows his head in approval as Sentry clears his throat. "Well I'm actually James

Cobblepot, but you all can continue to call me Sentry. I first used my powers while I was on vacation with my parents in Germany. We went to visit my grandparents and I was out looking for some fun of course. While I was out things around me began to look a little distorted.

"I thought it was just the drinks I had, but it was different. I don't completely understand it people began to move really slow…then I vanished and appeared directly in front of my parents. They both jumped and then the questions started. I was told not to do it again especially in public or else I would be taken by the government which I believed. I mean, what else would they do besides try to study me. I tried to keep it under wraps but then there was that one day in class… I kind of teleported above the teacher and floated there for a minute. Needless to say I had to leave town. I went to Chicago and found boss where I started my new life."

Landlord pushes himself out from the table finishing his bread he gets up dusting off his hands. "Well I will say this we definitely have something in common and we should try to build on that. We need to discover when it was that we first obtained these powers and who or what gave them to us. There must be a greater reason than what we have been fighting about."

Sentry and Titallic get up with Landlord; Sentry extends his hand towards Landlord as the two shake. "I doubt it, but I would like to know who or what did give us these powers. That part alone would be interesting. Right now the only thing that matters to us is winning back the boss's favor such that he won't kill us when we get our powers back. Even Arcos has been on his best behavior as of late."

"You guys are jokes," Ralph says while leaning against the doorway. He walks in chuckling as he grabs Titallic's bread eating it. Titallic stares in annoyance and shock while Ralph turns away walking back towards the exit. He stops for a moment turning his head back to the group of three, "Well I guess it is time to tell you about this awesome dude right?" Ralph says with a smirk as he swallows the last bit of bread.

Titallic turns throwing a plate at Ralph's head, but Ralph sways to the side avoiding it barely. "You ate my damn bread asshat!!"

Ralph shrugs before heading upstairs ignoring the three characters. He enters the control room finding Hawkins and Brainstorm upstairs working on the computers. "What are you two dudes up to?"

"Obviously getting this system to work, why do you ask? It can't be that you have any inkling of an idea as to what to do." Hawkins says with a snarky voice he runs his fingers across the keyboard accessing the backup files as words run across the screen.

Brainstorm scratches his head looking confused. "What are you doing up here Brainstorm it's plain to see you have no clue what is going on." Ralph says while hopping onto a panel sitting on the computer.

Brainstorm takes a step back, "I'm offering whatever assistance I can and getting to know Hawkins a bit better."

"To which, I don't know why he is really here. Whatever he wants to know he can just read from my mind...whenever he gets his powers back." Hawkins says with boredom, "More importantly, once again, Ralph you have yet to explain what you want."

Ralph laughs, "I'm just here dudes waiting for you all to ask the inevitable question. Who is this man, Ralph, where did he come from and how is he so strong."

"You were a thief that worked against the mob until you were caught. They took you beat you nearly to death and tied you to an anchor to drown you. You were sinking off the coast of New York when your powers first appeared and the anchor became as light as a feather. You surfaced and escaped only to go back and kill them all later crushing their bodies into the ground. Later on you were captured and detained by Monos and myself until you were released." Brainstorm says with his arms crossed, he watches Ralph stare in shock.

Ralph squints, "Like really dude ruin my story for your own ego what a douche."

Hawkins laughs as the screen shifts to a number of images. He stands up trying to sort through the images as the main entrance door opens. Katz and Albert walk in blood drips from Katz's sword as he wipes it off before sliding it back into his sheathe.

Tyreal stands around the corner his black suit wrapped around him he walks over to Katz. "Glad to see your back, what were you two doing out there anyway this is the second day you went out and came back with a bloody sword."

Katz scratches his chin with his eyes closed he begins to walk forward, "Come along we are going upstairs to Hawkins. As for what we have been doing, well today we leave this place and head for the towers. A more important question is why do you still have that suit on, I know about the other heroes from working with them. I know about Landlord being that he joined as soon as I left, but you Tyreal...you are something I have yet to study."

Tyreal steps up clearing his throat, "Well first off this suit is me and I am the suit. It was bonded to me about two years ago in an experiment. I was testing out a new cognitive amplifier that would allow people to control small objects attached to the suit by their own will when the computer overloaded and I was charged with millions of volts. The suit melted into my skin and slowly it became part of me even the metal appendages that I use now as chains. I survived and went into hiding because they wanted to work on me and try to pull it from me. Something felt right about it. Like it was natural…the next day I was able to retract it, and I was me…just like before. I am not sure it is alive, or if it is in me…but I am joined with it."

"So you're saying you really don't even have powers?" Albert comments as the three make it up the stairs. They find Ralph leaving out of the control room as they walk pass.

Tyreal looks down at his hands, "That's just it though they said it would be impossible for a regular human to survive that, and also the suit only gives me the ability to control appendages that are attached to it. You notice there is nothing attached. The chains come out of the abyss like the majority of my powers."

Albert stares confused with Tyreal, "So your powers come from an abyss what…are you dark?"

Katz comments, "Yet here he is taking all of that dark power and using it against me and my boys, isn't it interesting how that turned out. Anyway you may go and find Monos and gather the others in the cafeteria. We are leaving shortly."

Tyreal runs off as Katz enters the control room looking over to Brainstorm and then to Hawkins. "Well guys are you ready?" Katz says crossing his arms.

Hawkins shrugs, "Meh if you say you're ready then okay. I did get the computer running in some sort of language…it isn't anything close to the fifteen languages I know, but it's something."

Katz squints while walking over to the computer, "You don't have to rub in the number of languages you know Hawkins. Anyway yes Albert and I have scouted the surrounding area and we only found a few of the ferals around."

Albert nods, "Yeah, but even the few are dangerous. They are fast ambush attackers, you always have to be watching. The forest that we are going through is dark enough for the beasts to be roaming about. Such a large party will attract attention."

Brainstorm gets up from his chair, "So how long will it take to clear that area? If it will only take half a day it would be better to leave early tomorrow morning when the light comes in."

Katz bobs his head around, "That would be a good idea but it will take longer than that. Aside from that it doesn't matter how bright it is the trees are thick and they block out most of the light. All you can really see is the flicker of red from central tower. That's all we need to find where we will be going." Katz turns around looking slightly fatigued he leads the other three characters out of the room and down the hallway to the cafeteria.

Brainstorm leans over to Albert, "What's wrong with him?"

Albert shrugs, "What makes you think anything is wrong? Katz is fine…trying to take care of all of you can be draining you know, I'm sure he has it covered. What you should be worried about is how your team will fare out there in the wilds. This isn't like your pampered life back home you know."

"I know that," remarks Brainstorm, "You know you use to work with us just like Katz. You know we are good to deal with the wilds."

Albert laughs, "Haha just because I was around doesn't mean I was working with you guys really. I know how you all operate that isn't the point. The point is will you be able to handle this place? We will see I'm sure Katz won't let you all die that easily but still don't make this more of a burden for him than it needs to be or else I'll handle you all myself."

Brainstorm looks down in annoyance, "We aren't just a group of weaklings when will you and Katz learn this. We had you all dead to rights in Chicago before all of this, it has to count for something. When I joined the team it was just Katz and Monos. My powers made me a priceless addition so don't count any of us out. I have done the training for the others in the field. We are far better than you give us credit for and we have come a long way since you and Katz were on board."

Albert rolls his eyes turning away, "Time will tell as far as that goes."

They arrive at the cafeteria to find all of the other characters sitting around eating and chatting. Katz clears his throat, "Ahh well guys I hope you enjoyed your little break we are moving out in the next 10 minutes. I hope you all have gotten your weapons and armor from the armory if not you better make it quick. As for the food and what not do take some you will be traveling for at least a day and a half if not two days I think. Now I'm sure some of you have made new little acquaintances over the last two days, keep it up. I don't have the time, or the energy to deal with your bickering on the way."

Katz turns around, walking towards the exit he steps outside. The group scatters some rushing to the armory while others go and grab food. Arcos steps outside next to Katz he looks down to his leader.

"Umm…boss I just had a question and I want a real answer from you." Arcos says while rubbing his own shoulder blade. "Boss, back in Chicago you know I was planning to take over and run the group myself but yet you stopped those military lasers. You could have killed me then but you didn't why?"

Katz yawns, "You think I have the time and energy to entertain you with an answer to that hmm…"

Arcos stares at Katz waiting patiently while Katz looks up staring at his eyes again he smirks, "Ahh those eyes…still the same as the day I found you in that electronics store. Sitting there seeing me and trying to topple me then. Fresh with your powers you thought you had a chance. I will admit out of everyone that I've ever met you are one of the best with new powers that you just developed. Not many can catch me by surprise at first chance but that car to the face was quite a surprise. Though you still failed then and yet you continue to do it now even after failing how many times?"

Arcos closes his eyes, "Just three boss."

Katz responds, "Three miserable attempts to gain the power that you desire, that is why I keep you around. You will continue to work hard to become better, who knows maybe one day I will allow you to take control once I'm gone…but let's not lie and give thought to the wind. I kept you alive because you are part of my team if you died how much worse off would my group be? Aside from that you still have work to do and I expect it completed then you can die."

Arcos takes a step back searching for any hint of a joke or weakness he finds nothing before looking down at the ground, "Sorry boss…please don't kill me."

Katz closes his eyes flicking his eyebrows up he says nothing as the others come out of the building ready to start the journey.

Matthew Monos walks over to Katz patting him on the back, "This will be like the old days Katz are you excited?"

Katz quickly moves heading towards the forest he looks over at Monos. "I beg to differ this will not be like the days of an emotional wreck Katz due to your interference Monos. Instead I'm fully aware of everything and your dumb powers won't work on me again understood. You and Brainstorm are lucky that I am allowing you all to live." Katz strolls off standing before the forest he draws one of his swords.

Sentry slides up to Monos looking up at his peach colored face, "Well what did you do to piss him off?"

Monos shakes his head. "It is my fault and my mistake…when I first figured out how to use my powers I was working in a hospital with the emotionally traumatized patients as well as in the emergency room. It was there that I first saw my ability manifest. I was able to completely block or change their emotions removing them.

"When Katz first returned to the world I was there, I was in Chicago working at another hospital when he dropped out of the sky in front of me on my way home. You have never seen your leader like that, the way I did. He was so terrified I had to do something…so I blocked his emotions sealing most of them away.

"He followed me back to my apartment after that and I helped him gain control of what had happened. That was when I discovered he had powers too. We went on to fight against crime together, just small time crime though robbers and killers really.

"It was that time that we found Brainstorm, a teacher going by Richard Felton he was teaching high school in his home town of Lawrence Kansas. We found him on one of our nights out defending the city. He and his girlfriend were out when gangs surrounded them. Part of some sort of initiation or something, it doesn't matter though. We got in there and stopped them but not before Brainstorm came down with a massive stroke. Strangely though he got back up a short ways from the hospital and his powers instantly manifested."

Sentry squints at Monos, "Umm…you know I already know that. Or at least most of that information…he doesn't talk about it much, but he did hint at it before."

Monos responds, "Oh…well…that kind of kills my story you know. So I guess you already know about Brainstorm and my manipulation of his mind and emotions…blocking his memories, and making him work with us. It was absolutely the wrong way to go about doing things. I've learned a lot since then, and that is why I rarely use my powers before just sensing an attack."

Sentry shrugs, "Some sort of punishment on yourself? You should be proud to have been able to hold boss for as long as you did."

Monos shrugs, "I thought I could keep it going. With Brainstorm there I should have been able to hold him back longer, but when he broke free that was it. He swore vengeance and built his team...now look at us."

Sentry rolls his eyes as Hawkins walks by, "Haha you are fool Monos Katz would have gotten free eventually even if you planned around it. That man isn't one to be controlled that easily; besides you should be happy that you had that contact with him. That is probably the only reason that he hasn't killed you all yet, and the only reason he probably won't ever kill you. Now stop worrying about that stuff and let's get on with it."

Katz slides under a thick tree branch as the group follows along entering the dark forest area. Behind them a small gust blows dirt into the air while in the distance the soft hum of the tower can be heard as the red beam of light penetrates the skies.

Chapter 9: The Towers

Katz slashes down quickly cutting through a vine as he continues on the path towards the tower. The others follow along looking dirty and tired as they drag their feet through the brush below. Around them falling leaves and the sound of crunching in the distance rifts through the dense forest. Arcos and Titallic guard the sides of the group constantly looking out for eyes in the dark. The red light sparkles through the treetops directing the group forward.

The patter of feet ring in the distance as a loud howl comes down from above. Sentry turns his head upward to see a black slender cat like creature descending towards the group, its body covered in scraps of metal as its red eyes shine down on the group. Sentry takes aim lifting one of his pistols he fires it off quickly shooting the beast through the chest. The creature falls to the ground rolling down a hill as it dies. The surrounding forest growls as more eyes appear in the shadows.

Katz scratches his chin as Hawkins moves over to him. "Katz how far in are we? We have been traveling for a day so far and we have killed about a dozen of those things, yet that tower is no closer than it was before."

Katz grumbles, "We are getting there but even still this is quite far. We will need the full day to make it to the first tower."

The group continues on passing by more trees as the air grows colder and night begins to fall over the land. Several more ferals rise in front of Katz but he dashes forward cutting through one of them while Albert shoots another two with his rifle. Katz spins as one of the beasts leaps towards him he extends his sword out impaling the creature. They build a fire as they settle down to rest for the night each taking turns standing guard. As the night progresses more feral cats rise rushing in to attack the fire but they are slain one by one.

As the morning slowly arrives the group rises. After a short meal they return on their trek across the wilderness crossing over large downed branches and logs they make their way through the forest. The humming from the central tower grows louder, a short distance away a twinge of light peeks through the tree trunks and leaves as the group arrives at the edge of the forest.

Exiting the trees the group ends out in front of one of the large towers the black structure rises high into the sky, jagged nedles shoot electricity along the sides of the building upwards to the tip. Numerous lights flash along the tower's walls as Katz steps towards the main entrance walking up a long metal ramp. He then walks along the circular walkway around the tower to the opposite side where he finds a large metal wall with a small slit in the side. Katz takes one of his swords lining it up with the slit he drives the blade in causing the wall to open revealing a large door and a keypad. Katz nods in approval while accessing the keypad causing the door to rise above his head.

The others walk around the corner seeing Katz step into the building they quickly give chase running inside after him. The door slides down as the wall returns to cover the entrance. Inside the large tower a vast stairway circles around an elevator shaft. Upwards the tower opens into multiple levels each becoming illuminated due to the signs of life within the building. The elevator descends to the first floor as the characters hop on being taken up to the top of the tower. They pile out of the elevator drained and tired as Katz walks pass them and down a small pathway where he finds the control room.

He turns back to the group, "rooms are two floors down, I suggest you take the stairs. I'll be down shortly to get your capsules set up unless I can get them prepared from up here."

The others head downstairs finding the capsule rooms they each pick out their own. Katz remains upstairs tapping away on the keyboard checking the power levels of the tower; he accesses the sleep chambers activating the capsules. Later that day after the characters recover Katz enters the control room again. He looks out at the cameras seeing the sky bridge to the central tower he smirks.

"What has you so excited dude," Ralph says while walking in looking out the window at the vast forest and the plains out in the distance.

Katz responds, "We are getting across to the central tower then we will head home. Hopefully the controls still work over there and I can access all the towers at once. This trip won't be long at all."

Ralph snickers tapping a screen, "Umm…dude you might want to check this…there are some dots on it and it looks like a radar from those TV shows." Ralph says while standing over a screen.

Katz strolls over staring at the screen he rubs his chin as a frown grows over his face. "What are those…? Grr…" Katz walks out onto a large balcony looking out he sees two figures flying through the sky. As they come into view his eyes grow wide as his jaw drops. A man and a woman stop a short distance from the tower floating before Katz. The man appears in black and grey his black boots shine in the red light of the sky as he brushes his dark fingers through his black hair. A scar runs across his face as he smirks at Katz.

The female rubs her hands together with glee as her dark blonde hair floats gently behind her. Her short black cape sways under her hair attached to her matching black and grey power suit. She places her hands on her hips winking at Katz she smiles.

"No…way…I left both of you here to die…how are you still alive!?" Katz says with terror in his voice. "Bulla and Bertran…ghosts…."

"Hahaha nothing that simple Katz," Bertran says as he flexes his arms stretching his body. "You know we could have died back then but we have our master now and now we will have our revenge."

Bulla floats over stopping a few inches from Katz she stares him in the eyes, "That's right little man. You aren't as smart as you think."

Katz takes a step back while Ralph sits back watching the show from inside the control room. "Bulla, how did you get those powers? What did you do?"

"You'll find out soon enough. You're coming with us." Bulla says while reaching out to take Katz.

One of Katz's swords flashes across the air between Bulla and him as Katz stands back holding the blade with both hands. Bulla cocks her head to the side looking annoyed with Katz as Bertran dashes forward with amazing speed he grabs Katz and tosses him off the walkway towards the ground.

Katz flips over landing hard against the ground he stumbles to his knees. "With barely any powers this is going to suck."

Bertran and Bulla descend before Katz watching him rise slowly they laugh. "I thought you were far better than that Katz. Our master told us many things about you. Then again maybe the worm was wrong."

Katz jumps up swinging quickly he cuts through Bertran's clothing slashing through his black vest as Bertran moves back looking annoyed and surprised. Bertran holds his hand out from his palm a marble floats a short distance from his fingers. He slams his hands together around the marble clapping them loudly as he pulls them apart slowly. An axe forms from the marble expanding before his fingertips.

Bertran swings the axe with tremendous force smashing through Katz's sword and nearly cutting him in half. Katz jumps back reaching for another blade when Bulla leaps forward grabbing him by the arm she snaps his arm in two. Before Katz can scream Bulla delivers a tremendous blow to his chest and another to the back of his neck knocking Katz out cold.

Bertran walks over shaking his head, "Oh man…you didn't have to do it like that; I was hoping to cause a little more pain now anything I do won't be exciting."

Bulla chuckles, "He'll get up eventually. Anyway you take the body back to the master. I'll go deliver the message."

Bulla picks up Katz tossing him over to Bertran she takes off flying up to the top of the tower were she finds Ralph looking over the side. She lands in front of him as he takes a step back.

"Don't worry I don't plan on hurting you." Bulla says in a calm voice. "Actually I'm here to leave you with some instructions. It wouldn't be fitting for you to stay here and I know you want to return home. We can get you back to Earth all you have to do is bring us the soul gem of Sea Beast. His shrine is to the East of here. You will have three days to get it and bring it back here. We will take it from there."

Ralph nods in approval, "But what about Katz dude?"

Bulla's eyes turn sharp, "Don't worry about that mongrel we are taking him to our master would you like to come along as well?"

Ralph shrugs with a bored expression on his face, "Depends on how much you are going to pay me to go I guess."

Bulla growls back at him, "Nothing! Fail to bring us that gem though and you will meet the master personally and it will not end well for you. That is all your days start now."

Bulla rockets off into the sky flying towards the West as Ralph looks on bored. He sees in the distance a number of steeples and a large stone wall between them. He shrugs and heads back inside as Sentry and Brainstorm arrive in the control room looking for Katz.

"Where is the boss Ralph I could swear he was up here." Sentry says while walking over to the window looking out.

Ralph takes a seat again, "He's gone…taken by some people that he seemed to know. He tried to fight back it was pretty entertaining dude, though it didn't last long. I was hoping for a bit more entertainment from them. But on the bright side…ugh."

Sentry leaps across the room tackling Ralph to the ground he places his pistol to Ralph's temple holding him down.

Ralph looks up shocked and annoyed he raises an eyebrow, "What's up dude…you have an issue or something? I didn't even finish the story."

Sentry yells back, "SHUT UP! You let the boss get captured and you said nothing!! You didn't even try to help! I should kill you right now!"

Ralph's eyes flash and within the next second Brainstorm comes up from behind grabbing Sentry and pulling him back as Ralph scrambles to his feet. "Hey now you need to calm down dude. It isn't like your fearless leader is dead he's just a little tied up at the moment. In more important news we can still get out of here without him. We just need to get some creature's gem soul. Supposedly it is out to the East can't be that far away. We just need to get it within three days and be back here. Then those two that took Katz, they will let us out of here and back home. I can get my money."

A shoot rushes out of Sentry's pistol hitting the wall next to Ralph's head as Ralph jumps back shocked. Brainstorm tries to hold Sentry back as the others burst through the door hearing the discharge. After a short discussion and Ralph's explanation the heroes form a wall between Ralph and the three young villains. Ralph slowly slips away taking the elevator down while the heroes block the doorway. Albert walks over to Katz's team, "Guys get a hold of yourselves, while killing Ralph would be fun we have more important things to think about. Like how we are going to get Katz back."

"We will help you," Monos says stepping forward next to Albert as he looks over the three angered characters. "We will do whatever we can to see that Katz is brought back with us. We aren't leaving anyone behind here."

"Pff," says Arcos, "We don't need your help to get back our boss. We will kill them when they return in three days they might be tough when it's two on one but not against all of us."

Hawkins clears his throat, "Umm...may I suggest a far better alternative route than what either side has suggested? I say we go through with what they had planned. Whatever this beast of the sea is they obviously can't defeat it themselves even with their powers. This beast though must have some amazing amount of energy. If it can be reasoned with, then we are at an even better advantage, we can get it to help us and maybe explain what is going on in this world. Aside from that I would like the opportunity to find out more about this soul gem and what it does."

Monos nods, "That could actually be a good idea, we would need all the help we can get to deal with them especially without our full abilities. I say we split into teams one to go there and the other to stay here and try to figure things out. That way we can be prepared for when they come back...and Ralph will go wherever you all aren't going to go."

Titallic squints, "Why is that scared we will do something?"

Monos responds, "There's no way I'm taking that chance today.

The group makes plans as Hawkins gathers up supplies for the journey to the shrine. Elsewhere Bertran, Bulla and Katz arrive at a large black castle sitting in the distance it overlooks a valley and the towers as they land on a balcony. Inside the castle a heavy cloud of darkness fills the hallways and rooms.

Chapter 10: Dark Designs

Katz awakens in a cold black room looking around he sees a small flicker of light from the door in the distance. As he gets up he feels his arm noticing that it is fully healed; he shakes his head before getting off of the bed and walking forwards towards the light. He opens the door before him entering a dimly lit hallway

Katz squints moving slowly down the corridor to the next light dangling from the ceiling. "Where am I...hmm...Bertran and Bulla must have brought me here," he says to himself, "I'll need to get my location straight before planning an escape. Hopefully I can avoid them until I get back to my allies."

The hallway shifts taking twists and turns as Katz slides along the wall in an attempt to be stealthy. He arrives before a large steel door standing at the base he stares upwards at the massive gate as he scratches his head, "Well now...what is this...and why is it so huge?"

Katz feels along the cold metal searching for an entrance when he slides through the door falling into a massive room. Flames spark up along the walls illuminating the wide hall as Katz pulls himself to his feet looking around. He notices the flames leading upward to a large chair far away in the distance. Katz walks forward his eyes sharply scanning the room about him as he nears what appears to be a gargantuan chair two large red lights flash in the darkness above him. Katz staggers back hearing rumbles from before him as the ground shakes from a strange force surrounding him.

"There is no need to run Katz...for there is nowhere that you can go." The cold strict voice says from the dark.

The air becomes hot and sweaty as Katz breathes in the foul smell of death. Katz then takes another step back as a large black claw reaches out from the darkness slamming into the ground directly in front of him.

He notices the golden rings swirling around each claw. The black plated skin spirals upwards along the claw and into the darkness it vanishes as a head pierces forth above Katz. The two red eyes glare down staring directly at Katz as he stands still completely mesmerized by the gaze of the beast as another claw reaches out of the darkness wrapping itself around Kat's body seconds before the claw completely entangles Katz the room is flooded with light as Bertran and Bulla walk in from a side door. The light stuns the creature as it closes its eyes squinting from the brightness it jumps back to its seat.

Katz shakes off the powers of the beast gazing upon him for the first time fully his jaw drops in shock. Before him a long thick black tail sways across the floor circling behind Katz as it leads up to thick black scaled legs rippling with muscle. Several golden rings surround each leg while the massive long claws jutting from the toes dig into the ground in front of the chair. As Katz continues to gaze upon the creature he notices the heavy black plated scaled skin breathing slowly as its broad body fills in the entire chair small lines of crimson glide down the arms of the beast as its other claws also glisten with golden rings.

He stares up seeing the large black wings jutting out of the back of the draconic monster as his sharp head rests on the large scaly neck. Two jagged teeth pierce from his bottom jaw upward on either side of his face while his snout sticks out curving downward into a beak like shape.

"The light was far too bright Bertran; see that you don't ruin my gaze again! I will not stand for it. Now then…." The dragon says as it turns its sights upon Katz once more.

Katz turns attempting to flee when the tail of the dragon whips around him tying him up the dragon lifts Katz into the air and up to his hand. Katz lands in the palm of the dragon being lifted up to his face. Katz stands firm, crossing his arms, he attempts to show no fear as the dragon cocks its head to the side inspecting him.

"Who are you and what do you want?" Katz says in an attempt to be bold.

The dragon smirks as smoke blows from its nostrils pushing Katz back along his palm and into one of his claws. "Little man you dare to ask me a question. What I have seen is true you are destined to be my vessel. I am the beginning and the end, you may call me by my name though, Ragnor the dragon of war. As for you little man, you and I are to become one. You will lead me back to the world from which you come and I will help you to bring chaos to the multiverse. So will you work with me?"

Katz stares at Ragnor confused he steps forward standing on the edge of his palm a few inches from the dragon's face. "Now why would I want to work with you? I have my own team and my own goals least of all is this chaos that you speak of. Now that we have that settled I will be taking my leave."

Ragnor's eyes flash with a flicker of excitement as he closes his fist in around Katz clenching his body tightly between his claws Ragnor stares at Katz as his head bobbles around outside of his hand. Katz attempts to free himself but he fails as a smirk grows across Ragnor's face.

Bertran and Bulla fly up to the dragon's head they both float around Katz staring at him with pity. "You know you might as well give up and do as the master says; he is far more powerful than you will ever be." Bertran says with a smile on his face.

Katz stops, squinting at the three of them he grumbles lightly. "I don't have time for this. You release me now…"

Ragnor rises from his chair spreading his wings as they reach to the ends of the room he grumbles, "Now Katz you are hardly in any position to bargain. You have barely any powers by which to speak of and you are surrounded with nowhere to go. There is no resisting…why can't you see that? What is it that I've done to make you so upset little man?"

Ragnor bends down placing Katz on the ground he motions to Bulla. "Yes my master?"

Ragnor responds, "Bulla bring my pet in we need to show Katz his options."

"Absolutely my master." Bulla flies out of the room heading down a hallway while Katz hops back putting distance between him and Ragnor.

Katz shakes his fist at the dragon, "I'm not interested so just get out of my face, I'm leaving."

Ragnor speaks his voice causing the room to vibrate, "But Katz don't you wonder why it is that I have chosen you as my agent? You and I share the same desire you know what it is to be above everyone else yet shunned. Come now, I can give you so much more than ever before, my power is the greatest thing you will ever experience. And if you don't well there are other fates far worse for one such as you."

The doors open as Bulla flies in pulling a chain behind her. The sound of a heavy metal resounds off the walls as a large cage is dragged across the ground being pulled into the room. Within the cage is a large bird squawking loudly, the bird leaps around from wall to wall trying to escape. Suddenly fire erupts around the bird encasing it in a marvelous flame as the bars become hot. Bulla sets the cage down at the side of Ragnor.

Ragnor reaches down grabbing the cage with both hands he looks at the bird before turning his gaze back to Katz, "See this Katz? This was one of the beasts that watched over this land, now he is nothing more than a play thing for me. Whenever I am bored I take the bird out of the cage like so."

Ragnor opens the cage jutting his hand in as the phoenix ignites around Ragnor's claws but the dragon squeezes tightly forcing the bird to release its flame cloak in pain.

"Then I take the bird by the wing." Ragnor pulls one of the wings of the phoenix out looking at it elegantly before tearing it from the bird.

The scream from the phoenix echoes through the halls as blood pours out of the open wound. Ragnor stares directly at Katz who stands in shock with his mouth gapping open as the phoenix is dropped on the ground. Ragnor lifts his foot bringing it down on the phoenix he crushes the bird's bones.

Blood drains out on the floor as the phoenix dies before Katz. The dragon grins looking at Katz, "See what happens to my precious toys….you would be the most important of them all Katz. Think of what would happen to you."

Katz squints, "Ha you can only kill me once. So even if you do I'll be free of you shortly."

Ragnor laughs, "Little man…you know so little."

Ragnor turns to his chair reaching over into a small slot he pulls out a tiny crimson orb. The orb pulsates with energy as he moves the jewel across the room and towards the body of the phoenix. The jewel and the phoenix react instantly as a plume of fire rises into the air. The phoenix bursts forth from the flames completely renewed before it can fly away though Ragnor catches it tossing the bird back into its cage. He swings his tail around nearly sweeping Katz off his feet as Katz stares in annoyance.

The dragon looks back at Katz, "So you see little man there is nothing I can't do. I will use the power of this phoenix to raise you from the dead and continue to torture you for eternity unless you give me what I want. Toss him in the room with the bird. We'll give him a night to think over his decision…then tomorrow the fun begins."

Bertran floats over to Katz grabbing him by the arm he drags him down the hallway while Bulla takes the phoenix cage. The two are tossed into a large cold stone room as the door is slammed shut behind them. The phoenix radiates heat warming the room as Katz crouches in the corner attempting to think up a plan.

Later that night while Katz lies in the corner resting the phoenix stares at him opening its beak, "Katz, Katz." He rolls over hearing the noise he ignores it as the phoenix repeats itself, "Katz, Katz."

Katz opens one eye looking over across the room he sees the bird staring at him from its cage. Groggy and annoyed he rolls over when suddenly the phoenix bursts into flames heating the room instantly.

Katz jumps to his feet startled by the bird, he stares at it intensely. "What do you want bird?! Can I get a good night's rest?"

Katz walks over to the cage looking closely at the phoenix as the flames recede into the creature. The phoenix sticks one of its wings out to the side of the cage towards Katz as he reaches out touching it.

That instant Katz is blinded by a shimmering light, as he opens his eyes he finds himself on a plane of fire with the phoenix standing before him. "Katz I have brought you here for a purpose."

Katz rolls his eyes, "Everyone is dragging me everywhere for purposes that tend not to be in my best interests. And once again I'm sure I have no real choice but to listen to what you have to say as well. Go on."

The phoenix cocks its head to the side in confusion before continuing, "I know that you may doubt my intentions, but this is for both of our benefit. We must get you out of here before Ragnor takes it upon himself to obtain your body through other means. With it he can take your powers and use them to his own benefit. We can't allow this to pass."

"And so how do you expect to get me out of here?" Katz says with his arms crossed as he stares at the bird with skeptical eyes.

The bird responds, "The doors here are never locked; you must simply return to the throne room and grab my soul gem. It is the one thing keeping me bound to this body and this endless torture. After that you will take it into yourself and I shall be with you to free you from this place."

"Wait a minute…wait a minute," Katz starts, "You want me to go out there and grab some soul gem and do what with it, take it in…like eat it? Heck no, gems are rocks and rocks are not food. Aside from that if it is you then why don't you just call it back to yourself?"

The phoenix nods, "It isn't that simple. The soul gems can't be contained within our own vessels they require one choosen by to grant power to and I have chosen you. If you don't do this now, then you and everything you have ever held dear will die. Ragnor is not one by which to be trifling with. We thought so too when he first arrived here, and that cost us every last human on this planet and one of the three guardians in his first onslaught. He must be stopped at all costs."

Katz grumbles, "Hmm…grr….what do you know about this dragon?"

The phoenix squawks, "Not enough to be honest with you, he is old…very old, and powerful beyond reason, though when he first arrived we all thought differently due to his small size and the damage he had sustained from wherever he came from. We thought in his injured state he might need some help. The day he arrived was the day the sky turned black filled with some sort of dark energy, we saw him a human with dragon wings and other draconic features. It was strange at first but as the people gathered around him he rose with terror killing the majority of them and one of the guardians as well. If he can do that while on his deathbed, think of what he can do now. That is why the Kraken and I have held him here all of this time. As the remaining guardians we have done all that we can but now we need more you must do this for us."

Katz squints at the bird before turning around, "I don't know why I'm listening to a talking flaming bird but whatever." Another flash of light blinds Katz for a second as he appears back in the cell walking towards the door. Light floats in from the door as Katz cracks it open slightly with a surprised look on his face.

He travels down the hallway looking around for the entrance to throne room as he scouts the castle. Arriving in the throne room a while after. Katz tip toes through the area hoping not to run into Ragnor as he approaches the central platform. Looking up he sees the large chair of Ragnor and down at the side a red flicker coming from a spot near the chair. Katz hustles over to a smaller throne chair raising an eyebrow he looks over the chair to find a crimson sphere with a burning light within it. The light shines through the darkness nearly illuminating the entire room as he approaches. Katz quickly grabs it with both hands covering it in an attempt to drown the light.

He looks back up to Ragnor's chair finding no one there he breathes a sigh of relief. Suddenly the orb begins to burn against Katz's palms as fire surges up his arm and engulfs his body. The spherical gem begins to spin wildly circling around Katz with haste as it disintegrates into dust sprinkling itself above Katz.

The flames continuously burn over Katz refreshing his body as he breathes in the flames. His eyes become filled with flames as he hovers barely off the ground before landing quietly.

Katz hears his heartbeat, grabbing his chest he falls to the ground in pain black smoke seeps out of his pores creating a cloud of darkness around Katz; his breath quickens and his veins begin to pulsate. Blood drops from his mouth as he falls flat on the ground in constant pain. Seconds later he rises from the ground his eyes glowing red as he yawns. Bertran and Bulla walk into the room standing in front of Katz they stare at him.

"Did it work my master?" Bulla asks staring at the red eyes of Katz.

The dragon grins, "Well can't you tell Bulla, don't ask stupid questions. Now then let's get on with the rest of the days business." Ragnor walks through the halls in Katz's body having full control he enters the room with the phoenix looking at the bird with a smirk. "Very good job wouldn't you say partner?" Ragnor says to the bird with a spark in his eye.

The phoenix looks down, "Yes now let me out and release my soul gem I have completed this foul task."

Ragnor laughs, "Ahh yes your release as you would have it bird. He raises his hand, his eyes burning with flames, as he sets the phoenix on fire. The torrent of black flames engulfs the bird as it is being pulled into his hand. He absorbs the phoenix completely; an aura of fire surrounds Ragnor as he lifts his new hands creating burning wings behind him.

The blaze fades while Ragnor turns to his two companions. "Now that we have settled all accounts let's be off…the day is soon upon us, and the other fools will have prepared the way for my triumphant return. I'll get my swords there is going to be a bloodbath." The three characters fly off from the castle heading for the towers with Ragnor still in Katz's body as he smiles.

Chapter 11: Merger of the Sea Beast

A while earlier Hawkins, Ralph, Landlord, and Albert walk down a path from the towers passing by the forest they head down to a large body of water. They stand along the sandy shoreline looking out over the water as they try to find the shrine.

Hawkins steps forward, kneeling down he touches the water before turning his head back to the others. "Well hopefully you all are prepared for a swim…if it isn't on the shore or standing in the water it must be under it."

Albert looks to Hawkins, "Are you sure about that? It could be invisible or something. We have no clue what to expect."

Hawkins responds, "Well it is a sea beast by implication alone, it should be underwater if not on the water. Being that we see nothing on the water that only leaves one last possible location."

Albert bobs his head in thought while Landlord strolls along the shoreline looking out at the sea he shakes his head, "I wish we had better instructions…sigh."

Landlord stops kneeling down he touches the sand parting it in front of him when he catches a glimmer of green light from the corner of his eye. As he looks out he sees a line of green heading from the shoreline into the water.

"Hey guys!!! I found something!!" Landlord yells as the others hurry over. "Think this leads towards the shrine…where else would you see a green line sitting on water?"

Hawkins nods, "I guess so…onward we go then."

The four characters tread into the water moving slowly as it surrounds them when suddenly the calm sea becomes hectic pushing them further away from land; the water begins to swirl around them forming a whirlpool. The water pulls at the four dragging them under quickly, they spiral through a series of water tunnels. A few moments later the four characters get up looking around they find themselves in a large stone hallway drenched and cold they step away from the pond of water behind them shaking off their clothing in the hallway.

"Well great job you did there dude, now where are we…?" Ralph says looking directly at Landlord with an annoyed face.

Landlord retorts, "Hey it isn't my fault I was just trying to help; we wouldn't be in this mess if it wasn't for you in the first place Ralph!"

The two continue to argue while Hawkins and Albert shake their heads walking forward they scout out the area finding a large opening with multiple corridors leading different ways the two shrug.

Albert speaks up, "Well…this is going to be quite problematic…. Any ideas Hawkins?"

Hawkins looks over to his right and then to his left seeing nothing special about any of the paths on either side he points forward, "Why not just go with the soundest decision of going forward. There are only two paths that way I say we each pick one and go a ways down then we turn around and return here to discuss what we have discovered."

Albert looks forward taking the path on the right as Hawkins goes down the one on the left. Hawkins enters a dark passageway water drips from the ceiling as he walks down the winding stone path. He continues down the path mesmerized by the strange carvings along the wall, each shimmering with a soft green light. He takes a turn to the right following along the wall while Albert stops turning back towards the central room. Landlord and Ralph stop for a moment, wondering where the others went to they both travel down the passageway arriving at the central area as Albert steps into the room.

"Have you guys seen Hawkins?" Albert asks as the two just look at each other before turning back to him with lost expressions on their faces. "Hmm…he should have been back by now."

Albert begins to lead Landlord and Ralph down the path that Hawkins took when suddenly the ground begins to shake violently. The three characters are jostled around before collapsing to their knees as they try to stabilize themselves. The ground under them collapses dropping them perilously into a massive stone room below.

Water pours through the spouts on the wall falling into a lake below while Hawkins stands before the three characters, staring ahead he gazes at a cone shaped teal gem stone sitting on a pedestal. Further down a large tentacle crawls across the room snaking by the gem it curls around Hawkins. Another large meaty tentacle comes through the darkness slinking across the stone ground it slides over towards Albert. He jumps back as more tentacles rise from the water whipping around they try to grab the characters but the men bounce around avoiding them with ease.

The tentacles quickly withdraw into the deep water below as a fountain bubbles up before the group. Out of the water rises a large beast swinging forward. Looking at the creature Hawkins jumps back, the large armored shell on its back glows green and black as spikes run down its forearms. Two claws clap together in front of it while twelve tentacles wail around behind the beast. Its armored hide and elongated head stand before the four as it opens its mouth revealing rows of teeth spinning in multiple directions. The beast bellows blowing the characters back as it claps its claws together. The four stick like legs carry the creature across the ground dripping globs of water down under it as it towers over Hawkins and the others.

"No one disturbs my gem!" It says looking at the group.

Hawkins dusts himself off, "Guys the thing is large and ugly, I have no clue how I am going to get that gem with it standing right in front of me!"

The Kraken cocks its head to the side listening to the words its nine eyes squint, "Human…how did you get here this place is a sanctuary a grave of remembrance, how dare you desecrate it like the ones before you? I the Kraken protectorate of the Sea will not allow it." The Kraken says in a stern booming tone.

Hawkins nods to the others, "Never mind we have resolved one issue at least... the beast is crazed!"

Albert strolls forward, "Great Kraken hello there! I am Dr. Albert Alberason, and we are here to save our friend Katz. We just need to take this here soul gem thing that you have in your possession we heard it was in this shrine. So will you help us?"

"Dude I don't think that was a good idea," Ralph says as the Kraken's eyes become dark with anger and annoyance. The tentacles on its back shoot out towards the characters, in an attempt to slam them to the ground, but they each move quickly swaying around each of them.

Albert looks over to Ralph, "Well we tried the easy way; we are taking that damn gem one way or another."

Ralph nods, "I guess as long as I get some of the profits from it."

The Kraken pulls its tentacles up into the air, "You all have no need for my soul gem. I will crush you only the fools working for the dragon dare to steal from me!"

Hawkins grabs his axe from his back swinging it quickly he parries one of the claws. "Who is this dragon, and we are really just here for our friend? Of course I wouldn't give up a chance to have a look at that gem."

The Kraken jumps back roaring loudly it pulls it tentacles around its body creating a ball of water above its head. The Kraken then throws the water sphere at the characters slamming Ralph and Landlord against the walls while Hawkins runs up sliding under the ball and Albert jumps to the side avoiding it. Landlord gets up taking his rifle he fires off three shots at the beast.

The lasers blasts bounce off it's harden carapace. The Kraken rushes forward in an attempt to stomp on the characters while flailing its claws in a pincer motion. Ralph dashes forward with his sword he strikes one of the claws while Albert attacks the other grabbing it and holding it open with his bare hands. Landlord sails overhead raining down more laser shots while Hawkins jumps forward aiming for the chest of the Kraken he strikes at it with his axe. The axe slides across the Kraken's hide barely scratching it as the characters are pushed back by numerous tentacles slamming each of them into the water covered walls.

The beast smirks, "You all just don't understand what it is that you are doing do you? I shall give you this chance to realize just where you are and who you are dealing with."

Landlord struggles trying to break free as he looks over to Albert, "Can you move? This guy is too strong!"

Albert squints, "If I could move would I still be stuck here?"

The Kraken runs its eyes over the room watching each of them, "You all are here on orders to get my soul gem correct, but do you know what would happen if it is removed? The last line of defense barring the dragon would be released and he would be freed to ruin the multiverse. We, the guardians, are the last remnant of a long forgotten and ruined race. We once served and protected the human mates of the Cosmics, but then the dragon came and slaughtered them all.

"We tried to bind him after he killed one of us and we succeeded. He has been trapped here for millennia and now he has captured the phoenix...I am all that remains, now you will leave here and never return, live out the rest of your mortal lives in hiding. With any luck you will all be dead within the next year. I shall do what I should have done long ago and destroy the towers. There will be no escape for any of you."

Ralph's eyes become alive with fire, "No escape means no money dude. That's not cool!"

Ralph opens his mouth biting down hard he chomps on the tentacle shocking the Kraken. As Ralph slides out from the shocked creature he grabs his sword from the ground; leaping forward he slashes the Kraken across the face. The Kraken reels back in pain as the other characters are released from his grip.

Landlord runs over grabbing one of the legs he tries to lift the beast, Albert joins him and together they topple the Kraken knocking him on his back. Ralph and Hawkins both jump high bringing down their weapons together they cause a small crack in the Kraken's armored chest. The tentacles whirl around protecting the Kraken as he scrambles to its feet.

Standing back from the characters the creature stares at each of them. "You all are far different from those other two that work for the dragon. Those two retreated after the first water bomb then they tried to get here with the dragon's powers, but my shrine can't be entered by him or his mutated kindred. Nonetheless you will all die here today."

Hawkins rolls his eyes at the Kraken, "I shouldn't have to tell you this but we don't work for any dragon…in fact none of us have met this dragon of yours. Therefore you can stop this foolishness before you really get me angry."

The Kraken stares at Hawkins, "You dare to speak to me, a guardian, like that?!"

Hawkins responds, "Yes I do…some sort of guardians you guys have been, two of you have already failed and we are here near powerless and we're beating you. Regardless whatever it is you're so afraid of we can obviously handle it better. And as far as locking us out of our only way home well you are sorely mistaken. I'm going to take that soul gem of yours and I'm going to use it to my own advantage."

The Kraken laughs, "Hahaha brave last words."

Hawkins jumps back while the others blitz forward rushing at the Kraken they jump along the walls dodging the claws and tentacles while Hawkins sneaks along the ground heading for the gem pedestal. The Kraken notices Hawkins using all of his arsenal he bombards the field with water bombs and tentacle slams in an attempt to stop him but Landlord catches the guardian beast off guard shooting him in each of his eyes while Albert rushes in driving a hard punch to the Kraken's head.

With a burst of energy Ralph lunges forward thrusting his sword into the Kraken he breaks through its chest plate pushing the beast back slightly. Hawkins throws his axe as Ralph jumps off kicking his blade in deeper as the axe cleaves through the sword and smashes into the Kraken breaking his chest armor. The Kraken falls into the water as Hawkins reaches out grabbing the soul gem.

The light from the gem constantly flashes pulsating through Hawkins's body the energy radiates from Hawkins covering his body with a green light. The other characters stand back watching Hawkins as his eyes are filled with pure energy turning completely white as he stands still frozen in time.

The twelve meaty tentacles of the Kraken rise up along the sides of the platform swaying ever so slightly the straighten themselves holding in the air. The Kraken brings down his tentacles with tremendous force instantly shattering the ground and plunging the characters into the water.

Hawkins awakens feeling an urge to cause pain his body begins to grow as his muscles bulge and turn red. Feeling strengthened he clenches his fist as the Kraken circles around the characters opening its mouth it charges at Hawkins as he completes his transformation into Brutilus. Hawkins speeds back at the Kraken cracking his knuckles he slams his large red fist into the Kraken's face shattering a row of teeth as the Kraken is sent spiraling out of the water and into the wall. Albert, Landlord, and Ralph surface swimming over to the stairs they see the Kraken sliding down the wall severely injured.

The gem stone begins to resonate, spinning wildly before Hawkins as the Kraken looks on in complete shock. "Humans don't have these sorts of abilities…damnable abominations these are…the time of the guardians is now at an end…."

Hawkins swims over to the Kraken watching it sink he grabs the creature by the claw; he pierces through the water dragging the Kraken behind him. Using the Kraken's body as a battering ram Hawkins rips through a wall arriving in another large room of the shrine where he tosses the Kraken down. The beast tries to pull itself up but it staggers falling back down as Hawkins strolls in front of its face.

"Well now Kraken you thought yourself better than me, mistake number one." Hawkins says with a smirk on his face, "So what will you do now?"

The Kraken shifts each of its eyes onto Hawkins focusing on the cone gem in his hand, "You shall rue the day that you destroyed the seal. Nonetheless I am bound by the laws, take my powers if you dare human…whatever it is that you all are; you may be able to save your own souls from the wrath of the dragon with my powers…but know this. You will never obtain all of my knowledge. That will be your punishment for destroying the balance!"

The Kraken's body shrivels as a small portal appears on the side of the soul gem. The body is pulled in as the cone shaped gem shatters each shard of the gem darts into Hawkins's body filling him with more power than before as four large meaty tentacles grow from his back. The other three characters enter the room from a corridor seeing Hawkins in his new form they each take a step back. Hawkins turns towards them lifting his body with two of his tentacles, his eyes glow with a teal hue as he blasts all three characters with a beam of light.

As the light passes the three look around confused. "I just restored your powers you can thank me later." Hawkins says.

Albert takes off hovering in the air he smirks, "Good job Hawkins but where is the gem?"

Hawkins points to his gut, "In me…and that is where it will stay, I now have the power of the Kraken and better yet I can restore all of our powers. With them beating those two will be easy. Being that it took us two days to get here anyway we shall easily be able to return to the towers and take on the enemy."

Ralph and Landlord jump for joy as the four characters rocket out of the water landing on the shore. Taking in the fresh air they quickly head off towards the towers.

Chapter 12: Freedom

Hovering over the tower complex Ragnor, Bulla and Bertran stare down looking at each building they look down on the characters. Sentry and the others patrol around the top of a tower looking out towards the castle.

Sentry stops next to Monos looking out from the tower, "Well this is a fine mess we have here. Bertran and Bulla, I guess it will be good to finally see those two that caused all of this."

Tyreal leans over joining the two, "But who are they? And why did they want just him?"

Monos responds, "Bertran and Bulla are the two that attack Katz back when he was just the head researcher at Harvard. According to Katz, the government got wind of his experiments with atomic energy being pulled out of different dimensions. So those two were sent out on a black ops mission to retrieve the data and bring Katz with them. I guess if he didn't cooperate they would have killed him.

"When they broke into the lab late one night Katz was still there perfecting his formula. A small struggle ensued and one of them fired a shot. The bullet ruptured a holding tank for the high energy atoms. That caused the explosion back at Harvard two years ago, and that was when Katz vanished."

Tyreal nods, "Oh…I get it. They must be upset that he left them here, I mean it would only make sense."

Sentry responds, Yep, they weren't too pleased, but who cares. They have taken the boss and I will not stand for it. We will get him back and make them suffer."

"Foolish boy there will be no rescue today. In fact death comes to you all." The characters look up seeing Katz, Bertran and Bulla descending upon the tower they gather together preparing to defend themselves.

Arcos runs up to the railing looking out at Katz he notices his red eyes and his face paler than usual with cracks along his cheeks. "Boss what happened to you?" He asks.

Ragnor cocks his head to the side as he lands on the walkway, "Your boss, Katz is a little disposed at the moment. In fact I'm going to tell you right now he is in a dream, or rather a nightmare for him. One in which he is killing each and every one of you in the most gruesome and violent way possible. Actually I find it quite amusing haha."

Ragnor says with a hideous smirk on his face he walks over to Arcos, grabbing him by the neck, he lifts Arcos off the ground dangling him over the side. Arcos stares into Katz's eyes, seeing nothing of his former leader, he struggles to break free of Ragnor's grip.

"Struggling you fool, what makes you think you can defeat the dragon? I have no intention of killing you yet, assuming you have my gemstone, which you do correct?"

Monos steps forward, "They haven't returned with it just yet but what did you do to Katz?! I order that you release him now!"

Ragnor twists his head towards Monos staring at the man with a hint of annoyance on his face as he drops Arcos from the tower. Arcos falls quickly, but he regains his balance landing hard on his feet he stumbles around heading back inside.

Ragnor walks over to Monos staring him in the eyes. "You dare to give me orders…human…? You mortals know nothing and are useless so continue to bark and I will put the dogs in there place."

Brainstorm jumps towards Ragnor in an attempt to tackle him but Ragnor jumps off to the side floating in the air he laughs. Sentry leaps out in front, "What are you doing it is the boss we can't fight him not like this."

Brainstorm looks back to the others, "We don't have a choice, we need to break whatever hold is on him and I can't think of a better way."

Sentry shakes his head, "This isn't right…aside from that he obviously has some amount of power he will kill us!"

Ragnor scratches the back of his neck, "I'm tired of you all calling me that, the name is Ragnor the dragon of war and chaos. This body is just a vessel for me to use once I have achieved my ultimate desire it will be useless like the rest of you. Bertran, Bulla go and check the central tower. If the Kraken is gone and his soul gem taken you should be able to enter it now and open the portal back to your dimension." Bertran and Bulla bow before flying off to the central tower.

Ragnor cracks his knuckles before clapping his hands together as he pulls them apart out of his right palm comes the hilt of a blade, as he continues to pull the hilt from his hand a long thin blade is extracted. Ragnor spins the sword around with a smile as Brainstorm takes up his gun firing off three laser blasts at him. The dragon easily deflects each shot with his blade knocking the laser beams into the sky.

A black aura engulfs the beast as dark dragon wings spread out into the air. From the wings 6 more strange and exotic swords appear floating around Ragnor he laughs. "Let's taste blood."

Ragnor dashes to the top of the tower flashing pass the characters he slides across the walkway stopping pass Titallic. The characters all fall down as their armor shatters from a multitude of slashes. Ragnor gets up turning towards his foes he laughs. "Well that was far easier than I expected. Let's start severing heads."

Ragnor walks over to Titallic kicking him over he steps on his chest holding him down. He then grabs a long thick blade covered in sharp edges and grooves holding it over Titallic's head; he dangles the tip of the sword right above Titallic's nose.

"Let's see where I can make my first cut." Ragnor says with a twisted smile.

He clenches the sword tightly when he sees Arcos through the corner of his eye sneaking up behind him. Ragnor smirks standing still as Arcos lunges forward taking a sword in his hand he runs it through Ragnor's chest. The sword pierces through his body as the cold blade appears through the front of his chest.

Ragnor looks down at the blood soaked blade he turns towards Arcos, "Please tell me now….Arcos correct, haha pulling names from Katz's memories is quite exhilarating. Anyway what makes you think that ripping holes in my vessel would make me weaker…pitiful."

Arcos takes a step back as Ragnor takes a step towards him. Suddenly a powerful gale of wind whisks by knocking Ragnor from the building. Ragnor flips over catching himself in the air as he looks around annoyed. From the East Albert, Ralph, Landlord, and Hawkins appear flying over to the dragon they stop a short distance in front of him.

"Katz what are you doing? Where did you get that sword from and how did you get your powers back?" Albert asks while watching Katz closely.

He stares at Katz's red eyes completely confused as to what happened to him. Hawkins floats over to the other characters hitting them with a beam of light restoring their abilities.

"First off call me Ragnor not that weakling Katz he is floating around in depression." Ragnor says pulling the blade from his chest he incinerates it with a large black flame. Ragnor then blitzes across the sky attacking Albert with a swift slash.

Albert lifts his rifle to parry the attack but it is sliced in half as the sword passes through the weapon. Albert flies back circling around a tower as Ragnor gives chase firing off black fireballs at Albert. He spins around deflecting the fireballs with walls of wind he soars into the sky passing into the red clouds. Ragnor looks up annoyed he lifts both hands upward a blast of pure energy rises upward piercing the sky it hits Albert knocking him from on high as he plummets to the ground.

Ralph clenches his fist together using the full force of his powers he pulls Ragnor to the ground. Ragnor lands hard cracking the ground under him as his body becomes heavy. The others leap down from the building with their powers restored they quickly circle around the dragon.

Monos starts, "Brainstorm can you get into his head and separate Katz from this Ragnor?"

Brainstorm nods as his eyes become purple. He dives into Katz's mind in an attempt to find him as Ragnor grins, "What a foolish move for a mortal."

Inside Katz's head Brainstorm fall into a sea of darkness as he looks around trying to find an exit. In the distance a small light shines into the room illuminating one point across the dark abyss. Brainstorm looks up seeing Katz chained to a stone slab instantly flames engulf Katz and the stone resting on his body the red and orange fire attempts to break through the chains but it is forced back by a blast of darkness.

Brainstorm tries to fly out of the dark abyss but he feels something tugging on his leg. As he looks down a claw rises from the pitch black realm holding onto his leg it pulls Brainstorm deep into the abyss and into another chamber filled with numerous roaches. The disgusting creatures crawl over Brainstorm's body before he forces them off with a psychic force field. The roaches sink into the floor disappearing as the shadow of a large dragon rolls across the land stopping in front of Brainstorm. Ragnor stands in the distance large and muscular he stretches out his wings as black flames spew from his mouth.

"Ahh the psychic…how I welcome you to this realm…. Now then let's get to business. You want to try to separate me from the little man correct, and you think you have the power to handle one like me?" Ragnor says with his arms crossed as a chair builds behind him he sits down crossing his legs.

Brainstorm takes a breath, "You should surrender and release Katz. We won't kill you, but we will not allow you to leave this place."

Ragnor laughs loudly, "And what makes you think you can keep me here? Who's to say this isn't destiny fulfilling itself? You are in no position to tell me what to do. But I'll do you one better." With the snap of his sharp fingers Ragnor opens one of his eyes in the real world as Brainstorm tries to hold him trapped within the mind. "You can't stop me but you have awaken the little man. I shall allow him to see everything now he will feel it and it is all thanks to you. I'll let you die first for that."

With another snap Brainstorm is ousted from Katz's mind falling back he slides across the ground. Ragnor gets up one of his eyes becomes brown like that of Katz while the other remains red. Brainstorm gets up slowly, "We have to attack him now…we have to weaken him so I can get Katz out."

Blood drips down on the ground under Ragnor from his chest wound as he cocks his head to the side, "Katz said that really hurt Arcos hahaha."

Ralph's hands begin to shake, unable to hold Ragnor in his gravity field, he releases the dragon man to the shock and surprise of the others while Sentry, Titallic, and Arcos stand back shaking their heads.

"This isn't how I wanted it to be boss…." Arcos says as he stares as his leader.

Titallic closes his eyes shaking his head he walks pass Sentry and Arcos. His skin becomes metal as his body grows bulky and muscular. "You guys don't get it do you? If you don't battle him now there is no chance of us getting him back. We need to help do this!"

Titallic runs forward charging at Ragnor he throws a solid punch towards his face. Ragnor easily grabs Titallic's fist stopping his attack instantly he lifts Titallic over his head and slams him hard into the ground. Titallic discharges a mass of electricity through is body shocking Ragnor back while Landlord calls forth the earth spiking it upwards at Ragnor it hits him on the chin forcing Ragnor to stagger backwards.

From the side Tyreal rushes in delivering a hard right hook to Ragnor's gut spewing more blood from the wound. The dragon stops for a moment as his aura expands around him suddenly Ragnor unleash a wave of pure darkness blowing the characters away as twin horns break along his forehead rising towards the red sky. He stands fully erect with a smirk on his face as the characters pull themselves to their feet.

Ragnor flashes across the ground with amazing speed he drives a hard punch into Tyreal's gut cracking a few ribs he jumps spinning in the air Ragnor lands a strong kick to Tyreal's head knocking him over. Titallic jumps after Ragnor throwing two punches and a kick at him.

Ragnor easily dodges around each blow seamlessly as he slides into Titallic with a rising uppercut. Titallic is launched into the air from the blow. Landlord jumps in with a flying punch, but Ragnor ducks down avoiding the attack he counters with a blast of black energy from his palm knocking Landlord through one of the towers.

At the central tower Bertran and Bulla blast through the main doors walking in they pass through a long corridor while outside Hawkins jumps down from the walkway landing at the entrance. Hawkins looks in seeing the two walking down the corridor he follows after them. The three characters end up in a large room filled with machinery. Several computer displays adorn the walls around them as Bertran and Bulla quickly run to opposite sides of the room rattling away at the keypads.

Hawkins folds his hands while watching them as Bertran speaks up, "You done following us and are you going get this ready with us or not?"

Hawkins chuckles, "Tell me why I shouldn't kill you for abducting my friend and doing whatever it is that you all did to his mind?"

Bertran responds, "We took him for revenge and we probably won't even see that revenge take place if Ragnor has anything to do with it. As for his mind, that is completely fine ya know he's just a little preoccupied at the moment. But if you would stop wasting your time and help us we can get out of here faster. Or if you are feeling that sentimental you can go and try to save your friend from the master, but he will probably rip that Kraken soul from your body before killing all of you." Hawkins squints at the two while outside a loud rumble is heard.

Ragnor tackles Monos into the wall of the first tower shattering through the stone and metal he slams Monos to the ground breaking through the foundation of the tower. Monos tries to get up bleeding from his side he looks on to see Ragnor floating over him with an open palm aimed in his direction. A blast of black energy surges downward towards Monos but a wall of earth rises over him creating a dome it takes the brunt of the blast. Landlord slides through the hole in the wall jumping off the ground he catches Ragnor by the neck and tosses him through the remainder of the tower sending him rolling across the ground outside.

Ralph sets up another gravity trap locking Ragnor to the ground with an intense force as Albert, Brainstorm and Titallic stand around the dragon. Albert and Brainstorm call down horrific bolts of lightning while Titallic blasts electricity from both hands zapping Ragnor as he tries to get up from the ground. The bolts of electricity force Ragnor down suffering in pain he roars ferociously before collapsing.

The three end their electric assault as Ragnor convulses on the ground, "Damn humans…who do you think you are!!!!"

The ground trembles as Ragnor begins to spew smoke from his mouth the black smoke swirls around his body engulfing him as the single red eye gleams through the black cloud. The smoke rises expanding over the area out of the smoke comes a large dragon claw reaching out it snatches both Brainstorm and Titallic while Albert barely escapes rolling to the side. The smoke is blown away as Ragnor appears in his massive draconic form towering over the other characters; he clenches his claw around the two characters. Brainstorm tries to wiggle free, but he fails as Ragnor begins to crush his bones.

"What did you do with Katz?" Brainstorm asks while steadily coating his body in a psychic barrier.

Ragnor laughs, "Oh that one well I couldn't get rid of my vessel so I placed him inside for safe keeping. His body is too weak to continue this fight but I'm perfect. Now let's continue.

Brainstorm shifts his eyes around before focusing his mind sending out a message to each of the characters. "Katz is trapped inside the dragon which means we can attack freely, no more holding back."

Sentry stares at the massive dragon, "Man he must be pissed. I've never seen anything like that…but Brainstorm has a point, boss won't be pleased that we did nothing."

Arcos nods in approval while Titallic looks over to Brainstorm, "Hit me with all the lightning you can muster I have a plan to get us out of this."

Brainstorm nods calling down another bolt of lightning he strikes Titallic. Titallic channels the lightning through his metal body combining it with his own electricity he releases a massive surge through Ragnor's claw and up into his body. Ragnor drops the two characters as he staggers back whipping his tail around he topples one of the towers.

Suddenly the other towers activate sending waves of energy through the sky bridge as the red beam of energy dissipates leaving a large hole in the sky. The rocks along the ground begin to rumble jumping about as a loud hum comes from the gargantuan central tower. Ragnor turns his head towards the door with glee when he sees Hawkins walking out the front doors dragging his tentacles behind him. Ragnor looks down at him with hunger in his eyes. "The powers of the Kraken will be mine as well, now give them to me."

"You want it I see, well that probably won't be happening but you can try. I don't have a lot of time to waste on you though so you better make it quick." Hawkins says while crossing his arms.

Ragnor squints annoyed with Hawkins he slings his tail at him. The tail catches Hawkins along the side smacking him into the air but Hawkins wraps his tentacles around Ragnor's tail holding on he tosses himself up rising above Ragnor's head. Ragnor opens his mouth spewing flames at Hawkins but Hawkins dives through the fire building up speed he clenches his large fist tightly as he drops down driving a hard blow to Ragnor's skull.

The impact sends shockwaves blowing through the area as Ragnor stumbles in a daze; he crashes into another tower causing an energy flux through the central portal. The ground under the main tower begins to vanish as a large black portal opens underneath the building.

Hawkins shakes his head, "You idiot, big bumbling idiot. Now we only have minutes tops to get through that portal before the tower sinks into it and it is closed off forever! Stupid dragon!"

Ragnor pulls himself up, "WHAT! Damn humans!"

The dragon flaps his wings creating a massive gale he blows Hawkins back. From the side Arcos, Sentry and Ralph dash in landing blows against Ragnor's armored hide. Ragnor begins to feel a tight pain in his side as his thick plated skin begins to break oozing out blood.

Brainstorm stands back attacking Ragnor's mind while Landlord lifts large boulders from the ground tossing them at Ragnor's chest. The two boulders slam into the dragon shattering as he begins to feel his grip on Katz and the phoenix waning. Albert flies up to Ragnor's face striking him with a kick before calling down a hailstorm slamming the large icy blocks into Ragnor's back.

Tyreal dives down from above with multiple chains floating alongside him he changes them into tendrils before sending them forward. The tendrils rip through Ragnor's body tethering him to the ground as Tyreal fires one burst of green energy into Ragnor back.

Ragnor falls down to one knee damaged he roars before spewing out black tar from his mouth. A large body falls out of his mouth as the dragon continues to cough in pain. "Damn it…ugh…no…not like this…ah."

Brainstorm looks around at the group, "That's it! Let's finish this now!"

The characters gather in front of Ragnor preparing for one last attack as the dragon stares at them rising to his feet he stands with his back against the sinking central tower.

The dragon looks forward, "It would seem as though I under estimated you humans…never again." Brainstorm fires off a psychic bolt while Titallic and Albert attack with electricity. Ralph traps the dragon in a gravity pit pulling him down as Landlord sends a wave of jagged rocks forward. Sentry, Monos, and Arcos speed forward smashing the beast after the blasts hit with heavy blows to the chest. Tyreal holds out both hands firing a blast of energy into Ragnor's face as Hawkins jumps from the ground up delivering a final uppercut to Ragnor.

The remaining tendrils break from the ground as Ragnor rises slightly into the air. Another blast of lighting from Albert and Brainstorm hit Ragnor disintegrating part of his body as the dragon stares down on the characters nearly lifeless.

"My…destiny…cannot be ruined…not…like this." Ragnor says as smoke continues to flow from his mouth covering the remains of his body.

The smoke suddenly explodes blowing chunks of dragon down on the characters and the land below.

Arcos rises first from the explosion looking around at the desolate area he sees the small remainder of the tower sinking into a large portal on the ground. He walks over to the tar spewed by Ragnor where he finds Katz covered in the dark goo and lifeless he grabs him tossing Katz over his shoulder. Sentry runs over as the others slowly rise from the ground.

"Is he alright?" Sentry asks while wiping the tar from Katz's face.

Arcos responds, "I think so…I'm no doctor, but I would think he would have done more to kill him if he wanted him dead. We got to go though."

"That indeed we do," Hawkins says, "Now that the power has been blown out of proportion I don't know where we will land but we need to get through before the tower does let's go!" The characters run forth stopping at the edge of the black portal they stare down at it with worried eyes.

"Say umm Hawkins how did you get this to work?" Landlord asks looking worried.

"Tff you of little faith. I had Bertran and Bulla help with it, the two aren't nearly smart enough to do anything but I guess they have had training from that dragon on how to get the portal to work. After they step through I recalibrated it to a different location in Chicago so we are good to go. Don't question my genius; you seem to forget who was in charge of science for Harvard before Katz came along." Hawkins says with a smug look on his face. He then jumps first leaping through the portal alongside the edge of the tower. The other characters follow behind diving through the portal. The character tumble through a tunnel of light within seconds they are all blinded vanishing into a wet abyss.

Arc III: BEGINNINGS
Chapter 13: Homecoming

Bubbles appear on the surface of Lake Michigan when suddenly Hawkins and the other characters surface floating on the lake in the dead of night. Looking out they see the bright lights of Chicago adorning the night sky.

Landlord turns around seeing Hawkins he squints, "You couldn't put us out anywhere but the bottom of the Lake?"

Hawkins shifts his eyes around before diving under swimming quickly for the shore. The other characters take to the air landing along the shoreline as well with Arcos still carrying Katz.

He places Katz down on the shore scratching his head Arcos turns to the others. "What are we going to do now...he won't wake up...?"

Albert rubs his chin, "Let's go home for now, maybe he just needs a bit of rest. At least now that we are back his powers will start working again and that nasty little wound will get better."

"That's a really far flight for the night Albert," Titallic says with a shrug.

"You guys aren't going anywhere far tonight. We have more than enough room in the penthouse, you can stay with us get some rest and we will see to tending to his injuries." Monos says while picking Katz up tossing him over his back he hovers off the ground.

Arcos leans over to Sentry, "Let's hope they don't try to kill us in our sleep or something fishy. We will need to be on guard, they are back on their turf now."

Sentry nods, "I know what you mean, I'll be ready if anything goes down."

Arcos looks over to Monos and the others, "Sounds good we will take you up on the offer."

Hawkins laughs hearing what is said, "I still have my place here so I'll decline the offer proposed. Now that we are back I have far more pressing things to attend to."

Tyreal looks over the shore and the city he turns around perplexed, "Guys how long has it been since we left? What a week tops...."

Brainstorm nods in agreement as Tyreal continues, "Well they sure did a lot of reconstruction in that time but I guess we will worry about it tomorrow."

The characters take off heading for the Oak Park district they arrive at the heroes' penthouse. After cleaning up they each head off to rest for a short while.

The day after Bertran and Bulla appear walking through the alleys of Chicago. Bertran stops in front of a subway terminal crossing his arms he takes a breath of air, feeling relief. "About time we finally got back to our own world aye Bulla?"

Bulla smirks, "Yes now back to our old lives working for the government I'm sure they will have many questions for us."

Bertran responds, "Haha do you really want to go back to that? It would seem as though we still have our abilities we could do far better things, and Katz is dead now."

Bulla nods, "You have a point Bertran what to do…hmm…."

"You will…find me a body…that…is your purpose," whispers a dark voice.

Bertran rolls his eyes as he grabs his marble bag. Opening it he reaches down pulling out a large black cube. He sets the cube down on a dumpster with a sigh. "Oh Ragnor what do you want?"

Ragnor responds, "Either a new body to hide in or for you to guard me until I can regain my full power. Katz is partially lost to me at the moment."

Bulla's eyes grow sharp as the turns towards the cube. Ragnor continues, "You didn't think my vessel would die so easily. He is just severely weakened at the moment. I just have to get into close proximity and he will be mine again."

Bulla attempts to crush the cube with a powerful punch but the cube remains unscarred as the dumpster shatters. "You would have us drag you over there rather than kill our most hated person, forget you! We are free to do as we please now, so don't think I'm going to waste my time taking orders from a cube. Let's go Bertran." Bulla walks off from the subway entrance followed closely by Bertran a pulse of energy rushes out from the cube but the two ignore it while taking off into the air.

"We are going to find where Katz is and kill him dead," Bertran says with a smile on his face. The cube of Ragnor remains on the broken dumpster sitting still it releases a pulse of energy before vanishing.

Tyreal awakens strolling out of his room he finds Arcos, Sentry and Titallic sitting in front of the living room TV playing video games. He quickly rushes over, "Hey what are you all doing with my system?"

Sentry cocks his head back, "Making ourselves at home at least until Albert returns. Besides we haven't played this one in a while."

Tyreal squints, "Just don't break it please."

"Like we would do that," Sentry says.

Titallic interjects, "Oh you might want to meet with your boss guy, something about it already being a month since we got back you know."

"What a month, we were only gone a week maybe a week and a half tops!" Tyreal yells as he runs out to the balcony climbing up the ladder to the rooftop he finds Monos and Brainstorm overlooking the city.

"Guys are they pulling my leg right now or are you serious about it being a month?" Tyreal asks staring at Monos.

Monos nods, "We saw it on the news this morning and Brainstorm has confirmed it, this is our home the same planet that we left just a week ago I think, but time is different there I guess. It has been a full month and a few days since we left. Things have not gotten better yet either."

Tyreal inquires, "How not? I don't see as much destruction as before, maybe us being gone was a good thing."

Brainstorm guides Tyreal over to the side of the roof, "On the news there were reports of a giant raccoon attacking Milwaukee and the cities heading down this side of the lake towards Chicago. The raccoon creature has laser vision as well and the ability to morph into other rodent family animals it would seem."

Tyreal rubs his shoulder blade, "How would us being here stop that, and why didn't the military simply take it out like it did us?"

"That is the question I'm wondering about myself," says Brainstorm, "With those missiles and laser weapons they should be able to easily subdue a giant rat…but they are barely able to slow him down, maybe he is immune to them. In any case we have our work cut out for us that will be the first task to attend to, arresting him and working to rebuild relationships with the government and the people. We need to let the world know that their heroes are back."

"I don't mean to interrupt but," The three characters turn around to see Landlord climbing up the ladder and strolling over, "Wouldn't that be a bad idea, won't they wonder what happened to the villains. We can't tell them that we have been working with them, that won't go over well at all. And if General Niesse is still around he will probably still want all of our heads on a pike."

Monos laughs, "While that may be the case; we can easily leave the villains out of any reemergence story that we will tell them. As for the General he may have come to his senses we just have to prove that we are better than that. Also I'm feeling a lot stronger since getting back from that dimension what about the rest of you?"

The group nods in agreement, "I think it might have been from Hawkins and that light that restored our powers. They seem to have amplified them to a degree." Brainstorm says while rubbing his chin.

Back inside the penthouse Arcos and the others shut down the game system turning on the TV they see a scene from a news report showing a large rat attacking a northern suburb of Chicago. Arcos drops the remote staring at the report along with the others in shock. Getting up from the chair the three villains walk over to the balcony looking out at the sky they launch flying off in front of the heroes as they blitz through the air heading towards the north.

"What are they doing?!" yells Tyreal as the others turn watching the three characters speeding through the air.

The citizens look up hearing a sonic boom they see three human figures crossing over the clouds, terror fills their bodies. Passing over the city Arcos leads the group towards a rising smoke pillar where they see a large rat stomping on a house and whipping its tail around wildly. The three dive down landing around the large rat as it stops sniffing the air it turns from the building towards the characters. The citizens all take cover running behind cars and other buildings as the three villains emerge standing before the beast.

"Scrat you damn fool transform back to your human form and let's begin the slaughter." Titallic says while pointing at the rat creature. It hisses before covering itself in a ball of fur.

The rat shrinks down to human size as the fur is pulled into his skin revealing a tanned man with black dome shaped hair; a little pudgy he crosses his arms while standing across from the three.

"What do you guys want," Scrat says in a nasally voice, "I thought you all were dead, but it seems as though roaches like you pests are hard to kill."

Arcos raises an eyebrow, "You sure are talking pretty big all of a sudden there Scrat. Did you forget what happened last time?"

Scrat takes a step back as his eyes begin to glow, "You guys aren't invincible anymore! Take this!!"

Scrat blasts a massive laser beam from his brown eyes strafing the ground towards the three characters as they quickly jump around avoiding the attack. Back in the inner city of Chicago Albert flies over to the rooftop seeing the heroes he flips over landing before them as they scramble around preparing to take off.

"Wait a minute guys what are you all doing?" Albert asks.

Landlord stops in front of him, "Oh well your friends took off towards the north. When I went inside to see what had them in such a fuss I found that they had been watching the news and I guess they saw the giant rodent beast attacking the city."

Albert's face becomes annoyed as he stands there grumbling, "Scrat...that damn fool is back."

Tyreal stops looking over at Albert, "Who's Scrat?"

He responds, "Well you all won't be saving the day this time I can tell you that much. Scrat was the last person to attempt to join Katz's team. No one knows where he got his powers from or how but Katz found him annoying and repulsive. It was his dome shaped hair that irritated Katz to no end. That and his constant need for approval. Scrat was always trying to be better than everyone else but his power set was better suited for spying or digging into sealed places. He has the ability to transform into a number of pests and rodents all of which he can control the size of, though he favors giant ones. He also has laser vision hot enough to cut through most anything from Earth at least."

"So what will you all do with him?" Tyreal asks.

Albert rolls his eyebrows, "Well they will kill him that was the mission tasked to them after all. Anyway I'm going to go see Katz now."

Albert jumps off from the rooftop landing on the balcony he heads inside while the heroes shake their heads wondering what to do. Arcos spins through the air striking with a high kick but Scrat blocks the attack with his arm being forced into the ground from the strength of the blow. As Scrat falls off guard Titallic charges across the ground running into Scrat like a freight train he rams him with his shoulder sending Scrat rocketing back and into a house. He crashes through the kitchen landing in the refrigerator.

Scrat pulls himself out drenched in milk and eggs he transforms into a large possum stomping down the road Scrat walks up to Titallic attempting to smash him into the ground. Titallic easily lifts Scrat into the air by his paw and tosses Scrat across the sky and into a bus. Sentry then appears on high diving down with maximum speed he strikes with a heavy kick.

Scrat spews out blood from his mouth as he wheezes in pain. His body shrinks back to his human form as he rolls over crawling across the ground. "Ugh…ahhh…guh…damn…dang it."

"What's the matter Scrat not feeling so tough anymore?" Sentry asks with a smirk on his face as Arcos and Titallic fly in landing around Scrat.

Scrat coughs up more blood as his eyes glow he blasts into the ground sending up a burst of dust and dirt blinding the characters. Scrat drills into the ground spinning quickly he morphs into a bat soaring into the dust he vanishes as the characters look down at the hole in annoyance.

"Damn it he got away!" Titallic says, "Now we have to try again…"

Sentry looks at the hole searching around the end of it he flies back up to the others, "That was some mighty quick dig. Scrat has gotten better at that it seems."

Arcos shrugs, "Well let's get back to the boss maybe he is awake now." The three rocket off amidst a sea of citizens staring up at them.

Sentry speaks, "Arcos what has you so much on the boss's side all of a sudden? Last time you were trying to dethrone him."

Arcos responds, "Well while we were in that dimension Katz and I had a discussion. I've been a little childish I'd say."

"If you say so," Sentry says as the three speed over the city heading for the penthouse.

Back at the apartment Albert enters Katz's room finding him lying still he pulls up a chair sitting next to his side he crosses his arms as he leans back in the chair. "Katz what are you doing?"

Katz rolls his eyes around looking at Albert he grunts before closing his eyes again. "I'm trying to lay here and pretend as though the world ended already such that I have nothing to do. If you must know Alberason."

Albert responds, "I knew you weren't still unconscious you need a better trick."

Katz looks at him once more, "It's sure working on everyone else that it is. Anyway I'm entitled to a break every now and again. What's the news?"

Albert nods, "Well Scrat is back I guess in our month and a half long absence he gained a little courage to go on the rampage. Though I don't think he will be breathing much longer if the three musketeers have anything to say about it."

Katz sits up confused, "Three musketeers?"

"You know your boys…they have really banded together since you haven't been around. Part of your plan?" Albert says as he uncrosses his arms and cocks his head to the side.

Katz squints, "No actually that wasn't even thought up by me. Regardless it is good to hear they are working even better as a team and being that I'm not sitting in a smoldering pit I guess they aren't trying to kill Monos and his bunch yet. Nonetheless let's get on to more important things, how is everything with your love interest?"

Albert blushes, "All's well I went to find her last night once we got back she was in L.A. I took her on a flight so we could discuss what had happened. She actually came here looking for me around the river a few weeks back. She just so amazing."

Katz yawns for a moment, "Well that is just peachy Albert, but enough love talk before it makes me sick. You may continue to go about the regular activities I think I'll take another daylong break."

Albert gets up walking towards the door he stops, "So…what happened to you back there?" Katz slides back under the covers only allowing his eyes to glide around the room as the rest of his face vanishes. Albert turns back staring at Katz as he murmurs, "Well Katz?"

Katz begins, "I was tricked by a vile bird, and now I'm stuck with it. When Bertran and Bulla took me, the dragon asked me to become his vessel for chaos and war. I of course refused but that wasn't good enough. I met a phoenix that was nothing but a dirty liar after absorbing his soul gem I was captured. I guess the dragon placed his soul or some form of his entity into the gem… it was powerful. So powerful, I could feel it coursing through me…and…it was amazing.

"There was something about that dragon that was ancient even older than ancient like mystic even. And I was under his control. Then when we were fighting against you all I could feel it and see it. The pain of your attacks hurt yes, but…well…"

Katz slides further under the covers, "I…I…was enjoying it. There is something dark and tainted about that dragon and it filled me completely. So much that I didn't care about killing any of you. I was giving him tips….I had some control of myself and I did nothing to stop him."

Albert walks over looking at Katz hidden under the sheets, "What could you have done really Katz?"

"You don't get it Albert," Katz says, "I could have done something but instead I embraced it…and even now I feel that darkness around me…it is close and getting closer…and I doubt that I'd resist it again at all."

Albert shakes his head, "Well then we will have to make sure you don't have a relapse Katz. Oh and by the way I'm sure you are probably aware but Brainstorm undoubtedly knows that you are awake. How long will he keep it to himself though that is up in the air. You are far stronger than you want to give yourself credit for I think, don't sell yourself short Katz." Albert leaves the room while Katz stays in the bed; poking his eyes out from under the covers, he stares up at the ceiling.

Chapter 14: Strike Three

Late in the afternoon on the next day Katz steps out of his room looking completely refreshed he stretches his arms as he makes his way down the hallway and into the living room.

As he rounds the corner the eyes of his three villains glow brightly as they jump up. "Boss!!!! You're awake!" Sentry yells as they charge over to the thin man.

Katz takes a step back barely avoiding the three as his eyes grow wide, "Easy now boys don't rush grandpa now."

"When did you get up boss, and how are you feeling?" Titallic says.

Katz rolls his eyes hovering off the ground he floats before the characters as they head back into the living room. "I'm perfectly fine as far as you all should be concerned and I've been up for a while now. You forget who it is that is your leader. Anyway what has been going on with you all, I heard about your little run in with Scrat did you kill him?"

The three look down in shame as Arcos speaks up, "Not really…boss…he kind of got away and he hasn't show up again since."

Katz shrugs, "Oh well that happens. I wouldn't worry too much about it. Where are Monos and the others?"

Titallic responds, "Tyreal is in the back in his room and the other three are out. We haven't heard word from Ralph or Hawkins since we got back though. You would think Ralph would be by for his money but I guess he may have had a change of heart."

Katz responds, "Ralph has direct deposit set up I can assure you of that. But not to worry we will find him again eventually. Now then we have far more pressing matters to attend to. We need to get a new home. The tower plan must thus be accelerated."

Sentry looks over at Titallic and Arcos before turning back to Katz, "Um…boss I don't think you heard, but the tower over the water is sitting under another tower…yeah. When we came back the portal opened underwater and well the central tower came with us…haha." Katz stands still blinking his eyes at the three.

Elsewhere in an alley Scrat gets up covered in rags he rotates his shoulders attempting to ease the pain. He shuffles over to a dumpster, his body covered in bruises, as he lifts the lid looking for food and other things. Finding nothing rage fills his body as he picks up the dumpster pitching it through the wall of the building next to him. "Those damn fools are supposed to be dead!! This was my chance to shine, my chance to be the villain and here they are mucking up my plan, doh damn it! I hate them all!"

"Well Bertran looks like we have an old fashion cry baby here now don't we." Scrat looks around hearing the voice he turns towards the sky seeing Bulla and Bertran descending before him. The two land in front of him with their arms crossed radiating strength and confidence Scrat backs away.

He speaks, "Who are you two…and what do you want?"

Bulla looks over to Bertran before turning back to Scrat, "I'm Bulla and this is Bertran. We are sworn enemies of Dr. K.S. Katz and all of his little compatriots. Will you help us kill them?"

Bertran laughs, "Straight to the point Bulla I like that about you, always have and always will."

Scrat raises an eyebrow in suspicion, "How did you know where to find me and how do I know you are telling the truth?"

Bertran shrugs, "Well I don't think you could know to be honest with you but I'm sure you know that we are your best bet. Unless you want to put on another sorry show like the news has been showing on repeat for the last few hours."

Scrat hisses in annoyance at Bertran clenching one of his fists tightly he stares almost in a rage as blood trickles down from his fingers. "Say that again and I'll kill you myself." Scrat says with defiance.

"Hahaha," Bertran responds, "Oh don't get your tail in a knot. Besides you wouldn't get within a few feet before you were flat on your face. Well Bulla I say we try our old comrades maybe the will be more willing to do what needs to be done."

Bulla nods in agreement as Scrat comes to his senses, "Wait…no wait! I will help you as long as I get to kill at least one of them."

"Scrat my friend you can kill'em all except for Katz. He's ours," Bulla says with a smirk on her face. The three characters take off heading out of the city they move quickly towards the East as Scrat scratches his head puzzled at the destination.

A black cube appears from the destroyed wall watching the three as waves of energy begin to pour into it from the atmosphere. A smirk appears on the side of the cube as it moves into the sky. "He might do well enough for what I need, but I'll wait and see."

Bertran, Bulla and Scrat arrive at a base within Columbus Ohio; landing on the runway they stop as an alarm blares and soldiers surround them with weapons at the ready. "Freeze scum and prepare to be executed!"

Bulla steps forward as the soldiers ready their weapons loading them for fire. "You silly men don't seem to understand just who we are. Yes this weakling deserves death but us; the two of us have done nothing but follow orders from Commander Oliver all this time. Anyway you will find that your weapons will be of no use against us and that it would behoove you to find us the one in charge of killing the super humans like us. We have a proposition that they may find interesting."

The soldiers stand firm looking over at each other as one of them runs back heading into one of the hangars she gets on the phone. Minutes later she returns waving to the other soldiers as they stand down.

"Huff, huff, alright you have your audience, General Niesse will be available through the web chat session later today. You can plead your case then but he did say if it doesn't pan out he will have us shoot you right then and there." The woman says with a sharp stare eying the characters. Bulla leads the way with a smirk on her face as the three enter one of the offices and sit waiting for the conference call.

The screen before them lights up as static comes through the speakers, the black screen flashes brightly as Niesse appears sitting in a large room he stares at the three characters with annoyance. "What do you freak scum want with me?" Niesse says with disgust.

Bulla taps her fingers along the table while leaning back in the chair, "Well General Niesse it's quite simple actually. We need you to help us kill Katz and his band of fools. All you have to do is stay out of our way and divert the others from Katz himself. We can easily beat him in a two on one. Scrat here will assist in dealing with the others while we take on the main prize. After all is done you can claim the victory and at least look presentable since you did screw up killing them in the first place."

Niesse crushes a glass in his hand as his temper flares holding his composure he fumes from the mouth. "Hmm…an intriguing deal…huff. But what makes you think we can't handle them. Our weapons worked before we just need a more concentrated attack. With sheer numbers and force we will have them beaten easily."

Bertran interjects, "I don't think you fully understand how powerful those people are. Ten of them alone defeated our master and he was far beyond anything that you all could muster. We know how best to deal with them and unlike you who rely on toys we have strength and skill.

How the military sure has fallen from grace since we were in it. Anyway the offer is on the table. You better act fast."

Niesse squints, "Whatever I'll loan you a small squad but to add to the deal I want their blood as much blood as you can get from each of them. If you do that I will agree."

Scrat looks over at Bulla and Bertran, "Hey wait a minute why would he want that?"

Bertran places his hand up massaging his skull in irritation, "Who cares as long as we get to kill them it is of no concern to me. Bulla?"

Bulla nods, "You have yourself a deal old man." As the image fades the three get up with Bertran and Bulla in the lead they head out of the building preparing for their attack.

While out over the lake Katz and the others stare over calm water seeing boats sail by. "Hmm…well this is certainly not the best situation at all. Though I think we may be able to use it to our advantage. We will take what came through the portal and augment it with what we have already. Prepare to dive. Sentry how long before dark arrives?"

Sentry looks up at the sky, "Umm…about an hour and a half boss. Shall we wait till then?"

Katz responds, "Hmm…no, let's go now. The traffic on the lake will die down now anyway, dive down quickly and let's get the set up done."

The four characters spiral down into the water diving to the bottom of the lake they find the large metal tower with numerous holes and dents sitting atop their own structure. Exploring around the tower Titallic finds a number of fish swarming out from the main entrance. Small sparks fly from the computer screens inside the larger tower as Titallic passes over them popping out the top of the tower he looks over at Katz.

Katz points directing the group to the floor of the lake they wrap their fingers under the side of the building as Titallic transforms the four men use all of their strength in an attempt to lift the larger tower. Pushing it slightly off the ground they begin to hear it groan and bend as the metal starts to buckle. They drop the tower while Katz jumps back scratching his chin. Pointing upwards they four fly off heading back up to the surface.

"Well darn…plan B." Katz says, "We will need to find Ralph let's go." The four launch into the air when suddenly a heavy whistling sound rings through the air.

The characters look around confused as the sky is rocked with an explosion knocking the characters back into the water as a jet rockets by. Bertran, Bull and Scrat dive after the four. The team looks around figuring out what is going on. Bertran tackles Katz driving him through the water while Bulla grabs Sentry and Arcos tossing both out of the lake and high into the air where two more jets launch missiles at them. Scrat ignites his laser vision blasting Titallic down to the bottom of the lake he pushes him further down drilling through the lake floor. A dimensional rift opens behind Katz and Bertran teleporting the two into a hotel hallway.

Katz rolls away dripping wet he looks forward to see Bertran standing up shaking out his hair. "Well Katz you sure know how to make an entrance. I see you've gotten better since our last little skirmish."

Katz squints as he stands up wringing out his cape. "Strike three…Bertran I'm going to enjoy breaking you."

Bertran thinks to himself, "I've got to get back to Bulla somehow for the plan to work. Or can I take him myself…." Bertran pulls out a marble from his pocket spinning it on his index finger he tosses it up energy covers the marble as it morphs transforming into a large particle cannon.

The cannon lands on Bertran's shoulder as he takes aim, "Good bye Katz!"

Light fills the barrel of the cannon as Bertran pulls the trigger filling the hallway with light as it rips through the rooms heading for Katz. Katz squints before placing both hands in front of him. The particle blast strikes a barrier of atomic energy deflecting off to the sides it rips through the walls of the hotel and through the air around it.

As the beam thins Katz lunges forward spiraling towards Bertran he lands a strong punch to Bertran's chest knocking the cannon from his hand and sending Bertran bursting through the other end of the hallway and into the sky. The light begins to fade as night washes over the land.

Katz steps out of the hole in the hallway walking on the air he hovers next to the building with his arms crossed. "Bertran are you sure you thought this through? I'm not the same as I was when you last saw me."

Bertran, ignoring Katz, speeds forward attacking with several quick jabs, but Katz sways around each of them seamlessly moving between the attacks he launches forward with a strong knee towards Bertran's gut. Bertran blocks the attack with his hand pushing back he grabs another marble clapping his hands around it he transmutes it into a long blade. Bertran spins around slashing at Katz but he steps back dodging the blade, suddenly from the swing of the sword a burst of wind rushes out cutting at Katz it shreds around his clothing and armor knocking him back into the wall. Katz pulls himself free as a sickly grin runs across Bertran's face. He begins to slash wildly in the air sending out multiple wind blades.

Katz attempts to dodge around the attacks before taking off flying away as the wind cuts into the building behind him. Bertran gives chase slashing away at the air while Katz accelerates, his cape whipping behind him, through the city. Diving downward Katz rushes into a subway tunnel passing by numerous people while Bertran breaks through the road above landing in front of him.

Bertran charges at Katz in an attempt to impale him but Katz twists to the side barely dodging the sword he gets in close to Bertran attacking with an open palm to Bertran's chest. Light covers Katz's palm as he blasts Bertran back through the subway with an atomic beam sending him crashing into an oncoming train. The train rolls off the rails on fire as Bertran falls out the back door sliding down the subway.

He gets up shaking his head as he looks around for Katz. "Damn scientist is pretty good."

Bulla dashes out of the water seeing Arcos and Sentry flying away from the oncoming jets she smirks. As she looks around searching for Bertran and Katz she sees in the distance a bright white light and an explosion from a building in the city. With haste she flies in just in time to see Katz and Bertran dive into the subway.

As she floats overhead she sees Katz rising through the hole created by Bertran and she rushes down tackling him into the street. "Not so fast Katz. We've dealt with your friends and now we will kill you. Revenge is best served with a little bit of blood on the side."

Katz stares with one eyebrow raised, "Huh…what…weirdo. Nonetheless I'll take both of you on and win."

Scrat stops firing for a moment looking down at the heated water and the red earth beneath he peeks around for the remains of Titallic. Noticing nothing he smiles giving himself a pat on the back before swimming up for the surface. As he swims a cold shock overcomes his body as electricity surges through him from below. Titallic rises up from beneath him grabbing Scrat by the neck Titallic drives him out of the water and into the air. "You just tried to kill a metal man with lasers….does that make any sense?"

Scrat stares in dismay as Titallic's body glistens in the fading light. "How I thought they would cut you and melt you into pieces...damn it again!"

Scrat's eyes flash suddenly blasting Titallic in his eyes. Titallic grabs his eyes allowing Scrat to go free. Scrat then extends his fingernails turning them into sharp claws he slashes against Titallic's metal body barely leaving a scratch he turns and quickly flies away.

Titallic shakes off the blinding effects of Scrat's blast before looking around locating Scrat he rushes after him at high speeds firing off lines of electricity at the rat. "That was a bad idea!!" yells Scrat as he continues to dodge around the electric blasts.

Looking back he fires off more laser bolts from his eyes but each deflects off of Titallic's metal skin failing to do any damage. Titallic quickly gains on Scrat reaching out he grabs his leg. Swinging Scrat around Titallic tosses him at full speed towards the shore. Scrat crashes hard creating a plume of sand, tossing debris in the air.

He struggles to his feet at Titallic slides through the air with a drop kick aiming for Scrat's head. Scrat barely avoids the attack as he steps to the side watching Titallic crash into the sand. Scrat blasts the shore with a powerful laser beam turning the sand into glass as he strafes the beach.

Sentry flies around dodging a hailstorm of bullets while Arcos turns back facing the three jets around him he snaps his fingers causing their engines to explode as they fall from the sky crashing into the water. Sentry nods before dashing directly upward. The two jets behind him turn, flying after him they rise into the atmosphere. Ice and frost begin to build up on the wings. Sentry teleports within an instant appearing behind the planes he rushes up, grabbing one of the wings, he tears it off tossing it at the other jet.

The two explode dropping out the air while Sentry flies off meeting up with Arcos. "The military is still at it I see. But Bertran and Bulla too, this is strange. We have to find boss," Sentry says as he looks out towards the city.

The two fly off over the lake while Titallic stands up around a sea of glass his metal body shows numerous scuffs and scratches as he squints, "Damn it. This is going to leave a mark when I revert...stupid Scrat."

Above he sees Scrat searching the glass beach, higher up Sentry and Arcos sail across the sky. Titallic bursts from the ground moving quickly he surprises Scrat with a blow to the face knocking him out of the air and into the water. Titallic then joins up with Arcos and Sentry as they head into the city.

Chapter 15: Darkness Rises

Bulla charges across the ground with tremendous force, she drives her fist towards Katz. He leaps back avoiding the blow as Bulla runs forward striking a car she rips it in two while sliding down the road. Katz juts out one arm gathering atomic energy he strafes the street with a high powered beam blowing Bulla back and through a wall as the street goes up in flames. Bertran bursts forth from the subway carrying his sword he slashes at Katz from below trying to cut him in half. Katz rolls through the air barely avoiding the attack as a section of his cape is sliced off by the wind. Bulla rises from the rubble seeing Bertran she flies over as the two circle around their foe.

"Well this is quite interesting." Katz says shifting his vision from one side to the next as he tries to keep track of the two.

Above Arcos, Sentry and Titallic arrive preparing to move in they notice Katz holding up his hand. "Not so fast you three, these two are mine and mine alone."

Bertran laughs, "You really think so Katz? Bulla double team." Bulla laughs as she slides behind Bertran the two stop in the air as a cold wind blows by. Suddenly with impressive speed the two dash forward blinding Katz with their speed. Katz watches around him trying to track down either of the characters when he is suddenly blitz from the side. Several hits crash into his left side as he rockets through the air. Bulla accelerates appearing ahead of Katz she plows her elbow into him sending him spiraling into the ground. The ground sinks in around him as he creates a crater on impact flattening a car in the process. Katz pulls himself out of the crater as a water pipe explodes sending a tower of water out from behind him. The water splashes over his face, rinsing the blood from his lip, while Bertran and Bulla stop in front of him.

Bulla bends down to Katz, "Ready for another blitz?"

Katz squints, "Nice move…fast too…very fast. Follow me if you can keep up and I'll show you real speed."

Like a rocket Katz bursts from the ground soaring into the air he blasts off heading north towards the forest park. Bulla and Bertran dash after him flying pass the other characters as they give chase.

Arcos scratches his head, "What is boss doing?"

Sentry responds, "I don't rightly know but this doesn't look good."

Lightning crackles across the sky as the black cube floats overhead tracking Katz and the others, "This is even better than I planned. Let's see just how much control I can exert over my old body." A red eye opens on the side of the cube as Katz falls from the sky rolling through a number of trees he crashes over a lake.

Bertran and Bulla land on the shores of the lake watching Katz gets up they laugh, "What's the matter can't fly anymore? Bertran ready another double team."

Katz gets up hearing his heartbeat louder and stronger his chest begins to burn with pain. He kneels down on the water breathing heavily. "What…is…this…ah…this…power…."

Veins begin to bulge along his forehead rushing blood through his body as his irises turn crimson. Bulla and Bertran dash forward circling around Katz again they push up walls of water around them.

A smirk grows across Katz's face as he stands up dangling his arms at his side and his head down. "Well now…I've had enough games. You want blood…then you will have it, all of it."

Bulla speeds out first in an attempt to strike Katz on the left side again but Katz reaches out grabbing Bulla by the neck, lifting her off the lake he begins to squeeze cutting off her circulation.

Bulla struggles in an attempt to get free as she looks down into Katz's eyes. "You didn't think you could get away that easily did you Bulla?"

Bertran takes his sword, speeding towards Katz he slashes at his arm in an attempt to free Bulla but Katz vanishes appearing next to a tree he slams Bulla into the trunk knocking the tree over as he tosses Bulla to the ground. Katz holds out one arm as black shadows cover his hand from the shadows a long jagged sword emerges the black hilt rests on his palm as Katz slips his fingers around the sword.

He dashes over the water cutting through the wind blades from Bertran. He spins swinging the heavy sword against Bertran's blade. Sparks fall across the lake as a crack appears on Bertran's weapon. Bertran slides back pushing off the water he lunges at Katz trying to impale him. Katz stands still spinning his sword he catches Bertran's blade at the side breaking the weapon in half.

Bertran stops staring in shock he drops the remains of his sword as he takes a step back, "What…is all of this…?"

Katz responds, "Oh Bertran can't you tell look at these eyes. I have tapped into power."

Bertran's jaw drops, "Master Ragnor…no…I didn't mean it master, please don't kill me."

He cocks his head to the side, "Ragnor…no fool it's me Katz but I have the power of that dragon, it flows through my bones and muscle giving new life. You will die."

Bulla tackles Katz from behind dropping him in the lake. The others descend from above as Brainstorm and the heroes arrive. "What's going on here!" yells Brainstorm as the heroes stop behind the three villains.

"I don't know but boss is acting really strange, I've never seen him use that sword before, it was one of Ragnor's." Arcos says with a chill in his voice.

Monos looks over at Katz and back at Brainstorm, "We need to see what is going on in his head, did we really kill the dragon?"

Brainstorm's eyes turn purple, "I thought so, but I'll find out…there is a signal coming from somewhere I can feel the telekinetic waves in the air but they are scattered. I don't know exactly where they are coming from, they do center around Katz though."

Bulla is tossed through the air as Katz bursts from the water jetting towards her he calls forth another sword skewering Bulla against a tree. Bulla screams loudly as blood trickles down the trunk of the tree from her chest. Katz cocks his head to the side staring at Bulla he puts two fingers over her mouth. "Shh now…you don't want to drain all of your energy yelling. You won't suffer as long. Anyway hold on for a minute. I want you to see Bertran's death."

Katz turns quickly speeding off through the air he slam his knee into Bertran's neck knocking him over, and into the ground. The two slide through the dirt as Katz jumps back holding out both arms releasing a beam of atomic energy. The blast strikes Bertran exploding in a large cloud pushing him into the sky.

Katz dashes after Bertran grabbing him by his head Katz dangles Bertran in the air. "Well Bertran it has been fun but this is where you die."

Bertran struggles trying to break free as he feels his body slipping away. Bertran looks down to see his legs dissipating falling into nothingness. Pain fills his soul as he yells losing more of his body. Katz smiles while Bulla pulls herself from the tree looking up in shock and fear. Bertran's body steadily disintegrates into dust leaving nothing but his head in Katz's hand. Katz then tosses the head high into the air firing off an orb of energy he destroys it.

Turning his attention fully on Bulla Katz rushes over stopping directly in front of Bulla he holds up an open palm an inch away from her face. Atomic energy spirals around his hand covering his palm before bursting forward. The blast engulfs Bulla's head first completely vaporizing it before it expands covering Bulla's body as the stream of energy continues deep into the forest.

The light from the blast slowly fades leaving a path of destruction and flames in its wake. Katz cracks his knuckles holding his head in slight pain he looks around for another victim.

"That's right Katz you aren't done yet taste all that is Ragnor and destroy everything." The cube says as its red eye glows intensely.

Arcos and the others fly in landing next to Katz they stare at his red eyes. "Umm...boss," Arcos starts, "Are you okay? That was a little intense even for you...and where did you get those swords from?"

Katz stares at Arcos when suddenly he darts forward ready to impale him. Katz stops a step away from Arcos, with the tip of his blade resting on Arcos's chest. Sentry walks over grabbing Arcos while the world around them remains frozen in time the two teleport as Katz stumbles forward before the other characters. Sentry and Arcos appear behind Katz as the heroes quickly move to restrain him.

Holding him down to the ground Landlord traps his arms and legs in heavy rock bindings while Tyreal wraps chains around him restricting him. Brainstorm dives into Katz's mind while Ragnor attempts to do the same using his powers to reconnect with his vessel.

As Brainstorm enters he finds Katz standing before a large black door. His face sits mesmerized by the door as Brainstorm runs over to him. "Katz what are you doing!!? Wake up!"

Katz turns his head slowly towards Brainstorm his eyes glazed over as he stares at him for a minute. He then returns to gazing at the door. "I...I can't...hold it...and...that bird...that devilish bird cannot be trusted...it's so tempting...I must open the last door."

He reaches forward as a wall of flames blocks him forcing him back again.

The phoenix rises from the flames standing before Katz it stretches out its wings shining in front of the fire it squawks loudly. "Katz you must heed my warnings! This door will allow the dragon to assume full control of you again. Allow me to help you expel it. It is the least I can do for what I did."

Brainstorm stares at the two of them in confusion as the door begins to slide open. Brainstorm places a field around the door barring it.

Katz staggers forward trying to reach through the flames for the door. "Brainstorm…move. I need this…I need all of that power…. Then you all can die."

Brainstorm responds, "You don't mean that Katz. I'll take care of blocking this gate. Bird can you purge this from him?"

The phoenix nods, "It will be done."

The entire area begins to shake as Katz grows impatient. "You will not stop my ascension into power!"

Back in the real world Katz releases a storm of atomic energy from his body shattering the earth bonds and chains as he takes off from the ground. While inside his mind the Phoenix erupts into flames trapping Katz in a circle of fire before streamlining itself through Brainstorm's barrier and into the large door. Seconds later the door erupts into flames being completely incinerated.

Katz continues to fly upward when his body suddenly pulses with energy; he opens his mouth as a pillar of black smoke twists from his innards into the air. The large column of smoke dissipates into the skies above vanishing as Katz falls from the clouds landing in the lake with a splash.

"AHHRRRR!!!" yells Ragnor, "Damn it, damn it, damn it!! Damn humans and that stupid phoenix. I knew I should have completely annihilated his soul when I had the chance! GRR…!!"

The cube floats up calling towards him the black cloud of smoke it spirals around him like a ring. "Haha well at least I have some of my power back. This wasn't a complete waste I suppose. Plan B."

The cube vanishes leaving the cold night sky as the characters comb the lake looking for Katz. They find no one completely perplexed and confused they head back to the Penthouse.

A few days' later Sentry teleports in to Hawkins's office finding him sitting back in a chair reading as his tentacles turn the page for him. Hawkins looks up staring at Sentry with a blank and bored stare before turning his attention back to his book. "Is there something I can help you with, and you know there is something to be said about your manners perhaps a lesson is in order."

Sentry steps standing over Hawkins's desk, "I know, but this is important have you seen boss lately at all?

Hawkins puts down the book scratching his bald head, "Oh Katz…yeah I see him when the news plays what he did 4 days ago in Chicago quite a site I guess. But other than that or in person no I haven't seen him since we got back. Gone missing I assume?"

Sentry rolls his eyes, "Yeah he has, and we haven't been able to find him for four days since that battle in the forest. We've looked everywhere that he could possibly be this is the last place, but obviously he isn't here. Do you have any idea where he could be?"

Hawkins laughs, "Haha oh you think I would have an idea where he goes? The man has the power to shift through dimensions and teleport around using those dimensions. He could be right in this closet or he could be hanging out on Mars in a parallel universe. I'm sure he will pop up when he wants to be found. Now what is the real reason you have come here?"

Sentry responds, "Well aside from finding the boss there is this other matter at hand. That tower that came back with us we need both you and Ralph to assist with that. Brainstorm is out working on Ralph but I'm sure he will want money…."

Hawkins responds, "And that is where I come in I presume? What makes you think that I have any money to give to you all? Let alone the thought that I would give you that money? Aside from that why don't you all just steal the money for him it is part of your motif isn't it?"

Sentry responds, "It's not that simple. Monos and the others are always watching. We haven't done anything bad since we got back. We need to get a base again so we can plan our assaults without them knowing everything! You should help you are friends with the boss after all…come on be a pal."

Hawkins sighs while picking up his book again.

Back in Chicago Brainstorm soars over O'Hare constantly scanning for Katz he picks up on a strange energy high above the airport. "What is that…so much power…." Brainstorm stares around watching the area closely as soft rain pelts down on his face.

Brainstorm rises into the high atmosphere watching the storm clouds form he scratches his neck in confusion. "What is it I'm sensing?"

Placing two fingers to his temple he tries to amplify his senses reaching out to detect a mind but the entire area is shrouded in a cloud of static blocking his abilities. The air grows tense as lightning bolts shoot across the clouds. The crackle of thunder rumbles through the air while

Brainstorm descends landing on top of the control tower he stares up as the clouds grow dark spiraling above, "I didn't hear anything about bad weather today…hmm…strange." The wind wails loudly whipping around Brainstorm as his cape flaps violently behind him.

Suddenly from above a black pillar of smoke descends twisting down from the sky the pillar strikes the runway smashing a plane in half. Fire swarms across the tarmac as the plane explodes. Brainstorm quickly jumps off the tower heading for the fire along with the fire trucks and ambulances. He calls down a torrent of rain pouring it over the fire in an attempt to quell the blaze.

From the center of the smoke pillar two large red lights gleam out of the darkness flashing towards the airport a hot breath comes forth when instantly flames burst forth from the smoke pillar destroying the fire trucks and melting a section of the runway. Out of the smoke appears a large claw covered with black scales and golden rings around each finger. Two large black draconic wings rise from the smoke stretching out across the sky as Ragnor emerges blowing the smoke across the field. Ragnor's body appears completely refreshed and bulky. His black scales run down his chest and abdomen stopping at a jagged golden ring around his waist. Ragnor whips his tail around slamming the spike ball at the end into the cockpit of the destroyed plane as he turns his attention to Brainstorm seeing him floating in the air shocked.

A grin runs across his black face as more smoke foams from his mouth. "Ahh Brainstorm you are the first to witness the rise of darkness. The dragon has returned to this realm and soon I shall have everything that I desire. Stand back less you crave death."

Brainstorm responds, "Ragnor how did you get back?"

The dragon speaks, "Easily I am the dragon do not believe for a moment that I would not have the power to embed myself in multiple hosts to carry my seed into this world. Now if you will excuse me."

Ragnor scoops up the end of the plane flipping it in his hand he tosses it towards the control tower. Brainstorm quickly flies off getting in front of the debris he grabs it deflecting it off from the tower the end of the plane crashes into a highway.

Ragnor cracks the bones between his fingers, "This is going to end badly for you Brainstorm…very badly. Let's begin."

He roars loudly causing the ground to vibrate as the people run covering their ears in pain. He then strikes his claws into the ground running on all fours he charges towards Brainstorm. Brainstorm flies back at Ragnor balling his hands together he slides up to the dragon's face striking him with a thunderous blow to the side of his head. The punch causes Ragnor to rocket rolling over he crushes three other planes as his large body bounces across the airport.

Brainstorm holds his hand in pain watching as the blood trickles down from his knuckles. "Man…what is he made of? Owww."

Ragnor gets up moving his jaw around he smirks, "Nice strike…but not good enough."

In the distance multiple aircraft speed forth rushing towards the airport while Ragnor opens his mouth blasting flames. The fire rolls across the ground engulfing a portion of the runway as it barrels towards Brainstorm. Brainstorm quickly swings his right hand out in front of him creating a wall of wind. The wind surges upward spiraling into a tornado it absorbs the fire twisting it up to the heavens while Brainstorm tosses psychic bolts at Ragnor.

The bolts dissipate into Ragnor's thick hide doing nothing to the dragon as he walks forward digging his claws into the ground before him with each stomp of his feet. He then calls down lightning bolts at him, but the horns on his head act like lightning rods collecting the electricity Ragnor swings his head sending a large ball of electricity at Brainstorm.

Brainstorm dodges to the side barely avoiding the attack. As he completes his roll Ragnor's foot comes down from above catching Brainstorm off guard Ragnor stomps him into the hard ground breaking the concrete with tremendous force.

Brainstorm's arm sticks out from under Ragnor's foot wailing about he tries to get himself out as Ragnor laughs, "You don't think your tiny little arm would be enough to push me over do you? Once I underestimated you but now I've come to see that you are only a threat when together. In which case I'll just end you one by one."

Picking up his foot Ragnor stabs down his long claws from his feet ripping through both of Brainstorm's arms as he wails in pain.

Blood gushes from the wounds as Ragnor lifts his foot reaching down he scrapes the ground with his claws as he picks up Brainstorm, "So when will your friends arrive? I know they have seen me with how quickly the news travels. Anyway let's end this."

Ragnor opens his mouth as Brainstorm looks down the dark opening. A red and orange light builds up from the back of his throat. Brainstorm sees flames surging forth rolling up Ragnor's tongue, within that instant Brainstorm creates a psychic wall around Ragnor's mouth.

The flames reflect back down his throat exploding down his esophagus and into his stomach the dragon collapses spewing smoke from his nostrils as he coughs choking on the fire.

Brainstorm crawls behind a luggage car taking cover as he looks up to the sky seeing helicopters and planes flying in from the East he raises an eyebrow. "Where are the guys...?"

As Ragnor rises from the ground still spitting smoke and ash from his mouth he is bombarded by heavy bullets from a Gatling gun. The bullets pound into his carapace doing nothing as Ragnor flaps his wings creating a gale blowing the helicopters back.

Another set of helicopters lands releasing a squadron of troopers. They fire off the new laser weapons striking the dragon from all sides the lasers deflect off from Ragnor's hide as he spews fire down on the people turning them to ash. A few soldiers circle around behind the dragon lifting up a rocket launcher they fire hitting Ragnor in the back with a powerful rocket. Ragnor staggers forward from the explosion squinting he lifts his tail high bringing it down on the soldiers crushing them.

Ragnor eyes begin to glow brightly while two jets soar overhead, he takes aim preparing to blast them out of the sky when chains rain down over him ripping through Ragnor and locking him to the ground. Tyreal bursts forth from a cloud of smoke descending quickly he kicks Ragnor in the chest forcing him back. Monos and Landlord fly over to Brainstorm helping him up while. Tyreal lands in front of Ragnor, flicking his fingers upward, he causes the chains to rise from the ground behind Ragnor in an attempt to impale the dragon again. Ragnor ignites the area in a field of energy surrounding his body he disintegrates the chains while blowing away Tyreal.

The dragon grins, "Ahh I see we have a crew here, good. Now I can show you just how powerful a god really is."

"Are you alright Brainstorm," Monos asks."

Brainstorm coughs holding one of his shoulders, "I'll be alright. We need to stop him now."

Tyreal nods, "We can handle it you just watch our backs." Tyreal gathers energy in his hands firing it at Ragnor but the dragon dodges with ease vanishing from before Tyreal. He looks around flying higher as the soldiers regroup. Ragnor appears behind Tyreal swatting him like a fly, he knocks him into a helicopter.

Landlord grabs Ragnor by the tail flexing his muscles he pulls trying to lift the dragon off the ground. Ragnor easily lifts his tail carrying Landlord with it he slams Landlord down breaking the ground with Landlord's body. Monos rushes in front of Ragnor striking him with several punches to his face but Ragnor stands firm watching Monos attack he spits a small fireball at the man incinerating him. Ragnor turns picking up a 747 by the end of the plane he holds it like a club smashing the plane against Landlord flattening him. The dragon holds his other hand over Landlord opening his palm he releases a column of energy raining it down on his foe. Landlord lifts his arms in an attempt to block the attack as the energy deflects around him pouring into the ground. Brainstorm stands far at the side holding out a psychic barrier around Landlord saving him.

Ragnor laughs, "Well that should be enough well roasted that one is…ugh…."

A sharp pain builds through Ragnor's body when from behind Ralph appears hitting the dragon in the back of the head with a helicopter. At that instant Ralph intensifies the weight of the helicopter altering the gravity around it he knocks Ragnor over forcing the dragon to fall face first into a wall. His head passes through a restaurant court in the airport as he hits the ground hard.

Ralph stops throwing away his ruined and burned suit he reveals his regular super clothing.

Anger crosses over his face as he stares down at the dragon, "You just ruined my vacation to Bermuda dude! I had two girls a room and everything and you did it. Ruined my suit too, what's wrong with you!? You know how long it is going to take to get a refund of this!?"

With a snap of his fingers Ralph reduces gravity around Ragnor to nothing kicking him into the air he launches Ragnor high before intensifying the acceleration of gravity pulling Ragnor down again. Ragnor smashes into the ground with a heavy slam only to be launched back up by Ralph.

Ragnor begins to feel his body loosing cohesion as his spikes begin to dissipate in the air. Ralph pulls him down once more, but Ragnor unleashes a torrent of flame covering Ralph in black fire. Ralph sinks into the melted tarmac as Ragnor lands on his feet.

Taking in all of his energy he creates a tremendous sphere of energy. The blast completely annihilates the area in a large mushroom cloud leveling the majority of the airport and killing the people around. As the smoke and light clears Brainstorm is found impaled on a large metal pole lifeless along with the other characters bleeding and bruised. Ralph crawls across the ground pushing off the remains of a ladder he stands on his feet looking around at the desolate death filled area. Blood drops down from his side as he stares down at his ruined armor and clothing. He crawls over to Brainstorm pulling him off the pole he drops Brainstorm on the ground.

Coughing Ralph says, "Brainstorm…dude…we…need help." Ralph passes out again as a cold wind blows by.

Drilling through the ground below a black column of smoke rushes away from the destroyed airport and into the city. "Damn it! I can't hold my body in this dimension…I need my vessel." Ragnor continues to tunnel through the city heading towards the downtown area.

Chapter 16: Transformation

Scrat kicks over a can while walking down a side street. He looks up to the sky watching the sunlight fade he pulls his jacket over his face as he walks down into the subway. "Well I had a good month of fun, back to being a nobody stupid Katz and his super powered loser squad. I hate them with such a passion. If only I had more power."

He rounds the corner walking up to the turnstile he jumps over the bar. His feet land on the ground softly when suddenly the entire area turns black. Scrat finds himself trapped in a void completely blinded he stumbles around lost in the dark. Two red eyes shine down from above gazing solely on him as a thick cloud swirls around Scrat strangling him tightly. Scrat is brought up floating directly in front of the eyes he looks around completely confused. "Umm…what is this?!!"

Ragnor chuckles "Don't be so frightened child. You mortals always have such crazed reactions. None of you have been like the little man of whom I do desire to retake."

Scrat responds, "What are you talking about and who are you!! Let me go!" Scrat fires his laser beams into Ragnor's eyes but they fail to do anything as the darkness wraps itself around his throat squeezing it slightly.

The dragon speaks, "Now child you seem to be unable to comprehend what I'm telling you. You should be honored to be in the presence of a god. You desire power, the power to defeat your enemies the ones that made you look like a fool? I can help you with that."

Scrat's eyes grow wide with anticipation, "How so? What can you do for me?"

Ragnor responds, "I can allow you to hold my power, all of it. It is what made the little man or as you call him Katz so powerful. And he only had one half of my power. I will grant to you all of it, my entire being if you will take it. I can guarantee that you will easily be able to defeat all of them and the world will fear you."

Scrat grins in excitement power finally I'll take it!!!! Anything just give me all of your power!"

The darkness begins to spiral in multiple directions as a heavy gale blows around Scrat. The red eyes vanish being absorbed in the black void as a pillar of smoke thrusts forward ramming into Scrat it slams him against a wall. Scrat struggles to break free as the smoke chokes him pouring down his throat it fills his lunges before moving over the rest of body. Scrat's skin becomes black as scales mold over his arms and face.

His eyes glow red shooting out laser blasts as horns grow from his skull. Scrat yells in pain as his muscles bulge shattering the scales along his body. His veins ripple while the black room vanishes completely filling Scrat. Black armor flashes across his chest along with sharp jagged arm pads grow over his shoulders. His nails grow slightly as black claws cover his hands. A blast of fire comes from his mouth as he passes out.

Katz sits floating near the bottom of an ocean while large fish and other creatures swim by. His body moves slowly pushed by the currents as his cape barely touches the ocean floor. Deep within his mind he stares back at the phoenix as the two sit across from each other. Katz blinks as the two continue to look at each other.

The phoenix starts, "Come on Katz we have been like this for days!! Are you ever going to return us to the surface?!"

Katz blinks again, "Why would I? It is far easier to stay down here and not kill my team than it is to go up there and slaughter them under the will of that dragon. Besides I have very little to do up there anyway."

The phoenix squawks loudly, "Liar! You know that you miss them; I don't know why you try to be this amazing loner type. That isn't you Katz."

Katz rolls his eyes, "Bird listen here and listen well. You have been trapped in here for a good two weeks or so. You can't presume to tell me what you know or don't know. And furthermore you can't really be trusted as you lied and got me in this predicament in the first place. Until I can figure out how to completely and utterly destroy that dragon we are sitting right here and meditating. Anyway while we have time run that by me again how it is that you came upon this Ragnor."

The bird sighs, "Very well. It was over four millennia ago. That was when he arrived, before that the Kraken, Wolf and I were watching over the human mates of the Cosmic beings. It was then that a rift opened and he appeared broken and beaten in a strange humanoid form. We were ready to assist him but as soon as he arouse we found out that he was far more than anything we had ever handled or seen before. With one wave of his hand he killed them all and shattered the wolf's stone killing him instantly.

"Ragnor attempted to flee but the Kraken and I worked quickly to seal him within the realm. The dimensional portal was shut down and Ragnor has been there since, until now. He built himself a castle and he waited patiently, what for I don't know…but I do know this you will never defeat him without my help. Ragnor is a being from the days before even this universe I believe. He isn't a god as he loves to claim, but he is beyond most of all creation. We the guardians of the humans were created by the children of the Divines, and they were some of the most powerful beings across the multiverse. For Ragnor to be able to destroy even one of us that easily puts him in a class of his own."

Katz sighs, "Or it puts you all in a class far below most people. Heck you said the Kraken was defeated by Hawkins without his powers from what I hear. Therefore you all were just given the illusion of power and you can't be that useful to me."

The phoenix shifts his eyes around thinking it over he looks down, "You…you…may be right…all this time."

Katz responds, "Bird don't even give me that, I don't have time for it. Back to thinking and what not, I'll tell you this though. I'll give you one last chance to not be useless but that is if, and only if I really need you. I'll handle the dragon on my own, but if I fail then you can prove yourself then."

Deep within a subway tunnel Scrat falls from a cocoon covered in slime and mucus he lands hard on the tracks hitting his head. As he gets up he takes in a breath of air filling his lungs he yawns. "Oh man…what a sleep how long have I been out," he says.

A voice comes from within his head, "One week and two days. Now that you have completed the assimilation of my powers you are ready to go forth and destroy the enemy. Though if you desire to obtain Katz it would be best to keep his little groupies alive and hold them for ransom I say."

Scrat growls, "I should kill them all as soon as I see them but I see what you're saying. How do I draw them out though?"

Ragnor speaks, "Easily Scrat think for a moment would you."

Scrat scratches his head for a minute before laughing wildly. He then teleports out of the subway warping across the states he appears in Washington D.C. directly in front of the White House. With a wave of his hand Scrat sends the large gate flying back ripping it from the brick, he walks up the path towards the building. Alarms begin to blare as security forces and secret service members scramble around.

Scrat steps forward walking towards the wall of armed men and women he smiles, "This is going to be fun."

The dragon grumbles, "This was not what I had planned when I said to think…but I'll take it."

The armed forces fire at Scrat filling the air with a multitude of bullets but Scrat continues forward as the bullets fall to the ground harmlessly being stopped by a wall of force around Scrat. Scrat opens his hand, standing still, he holds out his left palm to the crowd building up energy from deep within he incinerates the people with a wave of black flames roasting their bodies to dust. Scrat then hovers slightly off the ground floating forward, he blows open the doors to the White House with a single breath.

As he floats through the corridors more service members attack him, but every assault fails leaving no damage on Scrat. "Now if I was the President where would I be hiding at…hmm…better idea."

With a snap of his fingers Scrat begins to teleport wildly and instantly through each and every room within the building hunting down the President; he finds a middle aged man along with four service members on an elevator heading underground. Scrat quickly impales one of the service men with his hand grabbing his heart he rips it out before turning towards the other. He knocks the gun out of her hand. Scrat kicks her back damaging the wall as the elevator stops. He grabs the other two by the face smashing their heads together he straightens his hair focusing his attention on the President.

"Well Roy…ready for a little trip?" Scrat says.

The man with broad shoulders and thin arms stands up. His small stomach pokes out just a little over his waistline as his toupee sways around his head. His pale blue eyes stare into Scrat's red eyes seeing evil he crosses his arms.

Roy responds, "Now you listen here sir, America doesn't bargain with terrorist like yourself. We have a contingency plan for this type of thing!"

Scrat responds by grabbing Roy by the collar he lifts him up as the two teleport outside of the White House standing on the lawn. Ahead of them a number of tanks and police cars encircle the building. "Well Roy a fine mess we have here. Will they kill their own President to try to stop me?"

Roy wiggles around trying to break free when Scrat tosses him to the ground. Running forward he charges at the tank and officers. A tank fires one shell directly at Scrat it explodes in his face covering him in fire and shrapnel. Scrat comes rushing out of the explosion carrying the smoke behind him he flashes pass the officers grabbing the barrel of the tank he rips off the top of it. Swinging it around Scrat smashes through the officers and their cars crushing them all with the top of the tank.

"Enough!!!" Roy says stepping out from behind the wall he walks over to Scrat fixing his suit jacket and toupee he nods. "I'll come with you just leave the citizens alone!"

Scrat turns to Roy with a gruesome grin on his face. "You think I'm killing them for you? Haha I'm killing them because it's fun!"

Waves of fire burst from Scrat burning the crowd of citizens, officers and soldiers around him as he turns around grabbing the Roy the two take-off leaving the carnage behind.

Back in Chicago Ralph gets up still holding his side from the battle with Ragnor he walks into the living room where Albert sits watching the news with a young brunette. She slides in close resting under his arm while Ralph listens hearing the news play.

"Breaking new out of Washington D.C. President Roy has been kidnapped by one of the super humans. Though the being did not say where he was taking the President to we know that destroyed and killed many in order to obtain him. This blow comes on the heels of the assault at O'Hare that has crippled the city of Chicago.

"The question is now what will the government do and how much more can we as a country take from these mutated humans. As we speak the military is devising a strategy to counter attack. It is being led by War General Niesse and Admiral Wizencut. The two are working with others to figure a way to defeat them…."

The channel begins to flicker as the image is distorted. The screen flashes as the local news appears on the tube. Within the news room stands the same female anchor from earlier and Scrat holding her by the head. He stares into the screen watching the public as the city of Chicago stares back at him.

The anchor trembles as tears roll down her face. "Please….please…don't…."

Scrat tilts her head back, "Shut up and stop your whining. You think I have time to hear your cries and complaints. Now then listen up and listen well people of Chicago.

"This message isn't for you, not yet at least. This is for a specific few, Titallic, Arcos, Sentry and even you Albert. You all will meet me this evening at the center of Oak Park. You'll find me on top of the roof of Unity temple. If you all come before me this evening and surrender to my will I might spare your lives. Also I'll allow you all to take this useless president as a bargaining chip. As for the military well the life of your President and everyone else within this city hangs in the balance. I would suggest you stay out of it. Finally for you fools powerless as you are. If you value your life then you better run…this is going to be a messy night."

Scrat flies off breaking through the roof of the studio he passes out into the darkening skies.

The anchor sniffles still terrified she shakes while running out of the studio screaming. "I quit this is too many times in one year!!!"

Albert flicks off the TV as Emily looks up at him. Her soft brown eyes stare at him with terror and worry. "Is that who you were talking about this Scrat?"

Albert nods, "That's him alright but that armor and those eyes. Something has changed. I have to take care of this."

Ralph slides off the wall walking to the recliner he sits down still holding his side. "Well dudes that doesn't look good for you guys. I'm going to be busy tonight not dealing with that."

Albert turns to Ralph, "You know that this penthouse is in Oak Park and Scrat is going to be right down the road from us. Please tell me where do you plan on going?"

Ralph responds, "Well that's easy out of here. Really though dude I'm probably just going to watch it unfold. He isn't after me so I don't care."

"What's the plan Albert?" The three turn around seeing Sentry walking in from the balcony. "I heard it all. Scrat is getting bold he knows he can't beat us."

Albert responds, "Get Arcos and Titallic we are going hunting. Scrat knows he can't, but something is off that armor and those eyes. I think he may have gotten power from Ragnor. We have no idea how this will go but we will kill him no doubt about it. Emily let's get you out of here. I don't want you in harm's way."

Picking up Emily in his arms Albert flies off from the balcony while Sentry heads in finding the others he informs them of the news report. Below along the city streets cars and people scramble through the area running for their lives they quickly attempt to evacuate.

As the light begins to wane Scrat stands atop the Unity building. He looks over at President Roy listening closely he hears his stomach growl. "Starving there Mr. President?"

Roy stares at Scrat with contempt, "Yes I haven't had anything to eat all day! What do you really want with me?"

Scrat laughs, "Truthfully I didn't know when I took you. But then I thought it over, and I figured you would be useful when the military attacks. I can kill the best of your soldiers, and those super powered fools all in one swoop. Then the country and the world will be mine."

Scrat's red eyes flash with tenacity as Roy takes a step back. He looks out over the horizon watching the sun sink behind the land he shakes his head. Below them hundreds of people run by escaping anyway that they can.

Chapter 17: An Unlikely Union

Scrat holds his hand up to the sky firing off a beam of energy. President Roy scampers back watching the display of power from Scrat in the distance three shapes come into view flying high they spin dropping out of the air between the President and Scrat.

Scrat grins with anticipation, "Finally a few of you at least, took you long enough to get here!"

Arcos steps forward waving his hand in annoyance, "Scrat you damn fool you haven't learned your lesson yet."

Sentry laughs, "I'm just wondering who is going to be the first to take his head off. I'm betting on me."

Titallic interjects, "Want to make it a game?"

"Yeah let's see who decapitates him first." Sentry says as he cracks his knuckles. President Roy quickly runs into the roof access door speeding down the stairs he heads out of the building.

Scrat waves his hands at the group, "Hey guys aren't you going to surrender instead? It would be far less painful for you. Think about it, I'll be your new leader and together we can kill Katz!"

Arcos yawns, "Yeah…we would rather just punch your face in rat man. Let's go!"

Scrat lowers his arm as black flames rise around him, "Please try this will be exhilarating!"

Arcos runs off first charging across the rooftop he jumps at Scrat attacking with a flying kick. Scrat steps to the side avoiding the attack while Arcos spins quickly striking with an elbow. He blocks it with his hand pushing back, he forces Arcos off balance before counterattacking with a heavy punch. The blow forces Arcos back, as Scrat moves in for another attack a blast of electricity passes between the two characters. Scrat looks to his side only to be punched in the face by Titallic.

Titallic quickly swings again hearing the cracking of bone he strikes Scrat in the jaw knocking him up in the sky. Titallic then transforms into his metal body chasing after Scrat but Scrat flips over hitting Titallic with a flash of energy. Titallic falls from the sky breaking through the roof of the building he falls onto a table.

Scrat points two fingers down aiming at Titallic he begins to charge a beam when time begins to slow. Sentry rushes upwards to Scrat he knocks him in the face with a powerful knee pushing his head back.

Scrat fires off into the air missing his mark while Sentry grabs Scrat by his dome shaped hair. Swinging him around, Sentry tosses Scrat through a building. Scrat rolls through the walls slamming his back against a pillar he slides down on the ground. Sentry swoops down from the sky flying through the hole in the wall he charges at Scrat. The rat man quickly steps to the side allowing Sentry to barrel through the pillar crashing into a desk.

Scrat opens his mouth filling his throat with light he unleashes a beam of energy striking Sentry hard he blasts through Sentry's shoulder ripping through the building. Sentry drops to one knee bleeding heavily from his arm he cringes holding his hand over the wound.

Scrat stands over him with a grin, "Well…looks like you are out of the game!"

He extends his claws holding them over Sentry's head he drives his fingers down preparing to impale Sentry. A wall of psychic energy warps around Sentry deflecting Scrat's attack as he looks around hearing heavy stomping around him. A wall to the south of him shatters as Hawkins walks in waving his four tentacles behind him he stomps over to Scrat towering over him he looks down.

Sentry looks over at Brainstorm nodding, "About time…did you get the President?"

Brainstorm responds, "I did he's safe near the outskirts. I'm sure that is where they will find him. Now you stay here I have a battle to win."

"Well this is a surprise what do you think you're doing here?" Scrat asks while glancing over Hawkins, noticing the massive muscles around his body he takes a step back.

Hawkins starts, "What's the matter rat boy scared? Well you should be anyway."

Scrat shrugs, "No…why would I be scared? There is little that you can do either. Not to worry I'll deal with you once I'm done with them and the heroic fools as well."

Hawkins runs forth, "No you won't."

Scrat raises an eyebrow as Hawkins quickly jabs him knocking him back through the wall and into the street. Hawkins charges out of the building, breaking through the wall, he chases after Scrat.

He flips over sliding down the road he pushes off rushing back at Hawkins. Scrat glides under another punch from Hawkins rising up from the ground he attacks with an uppercut hitting Hawkins in the jaw.

Hawkins takes the attack head on barely flinching he drives a hard fist into Scrat's gut causing him to bend back in pain.

Hawkins grapples Scrat with two of his tentacles lifting Scrat into the air he pummels him relentlessly with both fist driving heavy blows into Scrat's armor. Scrat is punched high into the air rocketing upward he regains his balance with annoyance on his face. "Dang it! Doh! You will die!!"

Scrat rains down hundreds of energy blasts bombarding the ground turning the roads into a sea of flames. Hawkins leaps off the road, rolling into a building. Brainstorm drops down from above covered in a psychic barrier he tackles Scrat from behind pushing him down towards the ground. Scrat lands hard bouncing off the shattered road as Monos flies in from the side attacking with a flying kick.

The blow pushes Scrat back slamming him against a wall. As he falters to the ground numerous rocks sail into him pelting him back against the wall. Landlord then snaps his fingers causing the earth around Scrat to mount upwards sealing him against the building in a trap.

The characters all land around Scrat as he shifts his head back and forth watching the nine of them. "Ingrates! How I hate you so!" Scrat yells as he shatters the rock and earth around his arms pulling his body from the wall. He falters to his knees breathing heavily as a stream of blood runs down his forehead.

The dragon whispers, "Well rat child looks like 25% of my power isn't enough for you. Shall we boost you to 50% I think so."

Scrat begins to shake violently as his body pulses. His muscles increase as a tail sprouts behind him. Fangs begin to grow from his mouth as his skin becomes thick and slightly scaly. Scrat grins before blitzing across the ground smashing his elbow into Monos's face. Blood spews from his nose as he rolls down the road.

Scrat quickly turns seeing Tyreal he leaps after him. Tyreal jumps back dodging a punch as Scrat hits the ground causing the road to crack under the force of his attack. Tyreal counters with a kick, but Scrat grabs his boot lifting him up he slams Tyreal down hard dropping him into the sewers below the city.

Landlord and Brainstorm rush forth attacking from two sides with a flurry of blows; Scrat sways around each attack wrapping his tail around Brainstorm, he tosses him into Landlord. Catching them off guard Scrat unleashes a burst of black flames engulfing the two characters as they roll down the street.

Sentry, Arcos, and Titallic fly over blitzing Scrat. The three characters rise into the sky chasing after him. Sentry teleports appearing before Scrat he kicks him across the face stunning him. Titallic grabs the stunned warrior discharging a massive amount of electricity from his body, frying Scrat with hundreds of volts. Scrat engulfs himself in black flames pushing Titallic away with the intense heat.

As Titallic backs away Scrat extends his tail thrusting it forward with immense force he drives it through Titallic's body ripping through his stomach with the tail. Cold shards of metal and blood drip down to the earth below as Titallic stares in shock unable to move he twitches in pain.

Scrat pulls his tail out allowing Titallic to fall to the ground as he whips the tail in front of his face licking the blood from its tip. "Delicious." Scrat grumbles while the black flames surge around his body.

Sentry rushes in quickly he lands a heavy kick to Scrat's chest. Arcos flies in behind Sentry zooming into the rat man he tackles him while his body is engulfed in the flames. The two crash through another building and into a city square as Arcos plants his feet in the ground tossing Scrat overhead and sending him crashing into a light pole.

Landlord runs up into the square while Tyreal pulls himself up from the sewers. Landlord claps his hands together causing the ground under Scrat to open dropping him deep into a crevasse. A building begins to rock back and forth being lifting into the air as Hawkins stands under it lifting the 100 ft. building on his own he tosses it over Scrat dropping the building on him. The building collapses over the crevasse sealing it. Sentry strolls over still holding his shoulder while Brainstorm carries Titallic over to the group.

"How long is that going to hold him?" Brainstorm asks looking around at the others.

Ralph shrugs, "As long as my gravity field can hold him down there. Let's hope his strength fails before mines." Ralph sits down on a bench watching the fallen building as sweat drips down the side of his face. "This is stressful."

Landlord shakes his head looking over at Ralph struggling he attempts to churn the earth around Scrat forcing him further underground.

"How did you get here Ralph?" Sentry asks.

Ralph responds, "Well I came down from the sky dude you guys weren't doing so great and I figured I could win something with the free P.R."

The ground begins to rumble shaking violently as the road begins to crack. Steam rises from under the streets while pipes burst open spewing water over the sidewalks and roads. A torrent of dark fire rises under the characters burning each of them as they stagger away from the flames.

The building is split in two as Scrat rises with two large black wings behind him. His face covered in black scales, a slow growl comes deep from within Scrat's throat while smoke and falls from the sides of his mouth and nostrils.

He lands on the ground getting down on all fours he charges forward at a lightning fast pace. Scrat runs into Landlord slamming him down hard on the concrete. He roars stabbing Landlord with his claws he breaks the skin nearly piercing his heart.

A gravity beam strikes Scrat pushing him off of Landlord as more beams sail into him hitting his arms, legs and torso. Scrat stands on his legs trying to move forward he falls down unable to regain his balance.

Ralph passes by Landlord running in he delivers a solid kick to Scrat's face pushing him off the ground. "Those gravity rings of mine are each of varying gravitational pull. Try and balance yourself or even fight back now dude."

Ralph jumps towards Scrat nailing him with a heavy blow to the gut. Scrat reels back as Ralph begins assault him with a barrage of blows drilling Scrat through the ground with rapid fire punches. Scrat's body pulses with energy blowing Ralph back he fires lasers from his eyes burning Ralph. The rat lifts his body from the ground still unbalanced he struggles even to walk.

Behind him comes Hawkins catching him in a bear hug he lifts Scrat off the ground squeezing tightly. Scrat's bones begin to crack under the pressure while Hawkins continues to tighten his grip. He wriggles around for a while, still attempting to break free, when he suddenly quits moving completely. His eyes flash as a wall of force covers him pushing Hawkins away and into a steel pipe.

The waves of energy emanating from Scrat expand becoming more vicious as the other characters attempt to get in close to attack. The wave of energy burns their bodies forcing them back. Their clothing and armor begins to disintegrate as their skin burns and bleeds. Scrat continues to unleash wave after wave destroying buildings and blocks of the city with each passing minute.

The military arrives at the outskirts of the city. Jets rush overhead carrying large missiles while Admiral Wizencut hops in a tank heading straight for the heart of the battle.

Far away a sharp pain flows through Katz's body; he opens his eyes shifting them around the dark ocean floor he sees nothing. "Hmm…that was strange…something isn't right…I feel."

The phoenix appears flying around the bird lands in front of Katz. "We must go or else your friends will die. I can sense a weakness in the Kraken and if he is weakening then his vessel must be weakening as well."

Katz squints, "You mean Hawkins? Well I wonder who would be able to do that…."

The phoenix responds, "The dragon of course, you thought that hiding yourself would prevent him from finding a different host. He can use most anyone with super human abilities like yours or theirs. All you did was provide him the best chance to kill anyone who could stand in his way. So now Katz what will you do? Continue to sit here and pretend to accomplish anything or will you finally assist the only friends you really have?"

Katz closes his eyes once more the water around him begins to churn with energy within a second Katz rockets upward flying through the water with amazing speed he bursts through the surface in a torrent. Katz then rushes off flying at full speed the air booms around him.

Scrat begins to expand his field again when a large metal rod rockets through the sky striking him in the chest it launches him across the city planting him firmly in the ground. Albert lands next to the burnt and wounded Arcos. "You all have done enough for now. I'll hold him off you all need to recover as much as possible."

Arcos struggles to his feet in pain from the burn wounds he shakes his head. "Albert…you can't do it. Ragnor was strong before but now him and Scrat together they are far more powerful than when boss was possessed. You will get killed and your girlfriend will kill us if that happens."

"We can still fight…ugh." Titallic says sitting up holds his right hand over the whole in his gut.

Albert shakes his head, "Come on I'm second in command after Katz for a reason. Now do as I say, Also get Monos while you're at it. He hasn't done that much so he can still fight."

Albert takes off leaving the others behind he flies forward. Above him he hears the roar of jet engines as he comes upon Scrat. Scrat leans up pulling the metal pole from his chest he smirks noticing Albert. "Ahh Albert there you are. And soon we will have the full set. Seen what I have done with your little friends there?"

Albert responds, "Yeah I notice. I'm not here to play games with you Scrat the military is here as well. You can try me first or you can try them it makes no difference this ends now."

Scrat runs forward as his wound regenerates healing itself he jumps at Albert slashing with his claws. Albert easily steps to the side watching the claws cut down before him he grabs Scrat by the arm bracing it tightly Albert pulls Scrat in attacking with a powerful knee to his gut. With a snap of his fingers Albert calls the metal pole back to his hand. Pushing Scrat back Albert swings the pole with all of his strength breaking it against Scrat's side.

Scrat crashes along the ground yelling in annoyance while Albert lifts off flying into Scrat with a hard punch to the face. Scrat staggers back tricking Albert to going for another attack; he teleports around Albert grabbing him by the head Scrat flips Albert over his shoulder slamming him with a hard thud into a wall. Scrat then flashes delivering a hard punch he forces Albert to crash through the wall. Wizencut's tank drives over the ruined terrain seeing the two battle he begins to target Scrat.

Albert comes flying back through the broken wall but Scrat jumps over him grabbing his leg now Scrat swings Albert around before tossing him into the sky. Twin missiles rush through the grey clouds hitting the ground around Scrat as they explode doing no damage to him.

Wizencut fires the tank shell the shell crashes into Scrat pushing him back along the road. He dusts off his armor and turns his attentions on the planes. "What!!!" Wizencut yells as he sees Scrat take off. "That shell was laced with the new energy cell from Cadmus…damn it! We can't win this….if nothing works crap!"

Scrat chases after one of the jets while Albert regains his balance rushing after his foe. Scrat barrels through one of the jets destroying it instantly as he rushes off chasing the others. Albert holds out his hand pulling one of the jets backwards he slams it into Scrat stunning him as the jet explodes. Albert then calls down a bolt of lightning striking Scrat. The lightning pushes Scrat from the air as he topples across a rooftop.

Albert quickly descends pulling a missile from the final plane he drops it down on the rooftop covering Scrat in a large explosion. "Alright I think I got him at least for now."

Black tendrils rush out from the smoldering building wrapping around Albert. Scrat staggers out of the flames bleeding from his sides and his face he bolts into Albert tackling him down to the ground. The tendrils begin to burrow into Albert's body. He yells in pain, blood trickling from his body while Scrat stands over him almost in a trance.

Wizencut drives over loading another shell he fires at Scrat again. The shell forces Scrat back freeing Albert as it explodes. Scrat flaps his wings blowing away the smoke and flames from the attack as he turns his full attention to Wizencut.

"I'm so sick of you." He whispers while holding out his left hand pointing his index finger at the tank.

A solid beam cuts through the tank slicing it down the middle he cracks it open like a nut in a shell. Wizencut crawls out the left side of the tank looking out he sees Scrat standing over him with a grizzly grin on his face.

Scrat strikes down with his claws at the Admiral seeing the fear in his eyes while Wizencut watches as his life flashes before him. "I have failed." He murmurs as a cold gale whips around knocking both sections of the destroyed tank into the air.

A loud and heavy boom rings in his ears as Wizencut is forced through the air crashing down on a distant street he slowly gets up. He opens his eyes to see Scrat gone from sight. Scrat rolls hard bouncing off the ground for a mile long stretch he finally crashes into a boat house tearing his hand off as he slides over a propeller. Outside Dr. Katz stands firm his cape flailing behind him in the dark night sky.

Chapter 18: Resurrection

Katz cocks one hand out towards the damaged boat house gathering atomic energy at his palm, he launches a single orb at the building. As the orb touches the side of the bout house it erupts into flames exploding with a large bang. Ashes of wood and metal fall into the lake and on the shore while Katz stands still, crossing his arms, he stares at the blaze ahead. Out of the flames comes Scrat bleeding heavily and barely able to breathe he stares at Katz with contempt.

"Scrat good to see you, well not really. Did not I say that you would die upon our next meeting? And here you are not only aggravating me but trying to kill my boys. Grave mistake, poor rat man."

Scrat smiles lifting up his stump of an arm he ignites it in a surge of dark fire. The flame molds itself into a new arm. He responds, "You were the one who said I was weak. What about now!! Now I'm the one with the power granted to me for free by the lord Ragnor and I will prove to you tha-"

Katz fires off a long beam of energy striking Scrat in the chest he pushes him into the water as the beam explodes. Scrat floats to the surface wincing in pain when Katz flies over him, "Shut up!! I don't want to hear your mouth!"

Katz unleashes a burst of energy exploding it at point blank range in Scrat's face. He accelerates hitting the bottom of the lake while Katz floats through the cloud of smoke and flame from the blast unscathed.

"Well rat man you have reached the end of your rope." Ragnor says deep within Scrat's mind darkness swirls around his astral body. The tail of the dragon wraps around him as Ragnor sits at his side.

"What do you mean?" Scrat asks, "I can still fight more power is all I need."

Ragnor smirks looking at Scrat with his deep red eyes, "Ahh but that is where you are wrong. I allowed you time to play with them and I even thought about allowing you a shot at Katz, but in your current state you are pitiful nearly useless. You don't understand the intricacies of power. Your only purpose in this life was to draw out the one that I desired. You have accomplished that goal and now I will take command. Do not worry though, I will make your death as painful as possible. You were a useless host, but I can still make your body and your tolerance of my dark powers useful to me."

Scrat begins to cringe as Ragnor grabs him by the head drilling his claws through his skull. He yells in pain before falling silent, bubbles escape his open mouth.

The lake begins to churn and spin as the water bubbles Katz stares down as Scrat's body rises from the lake the color missing from his face and skin he floats upwards stopping directly across from Katz. The black armor slims as the spiked armor completely molds itself to his body. The spikes retract along with his wings. His muscles shrink and his horns twist upward from his forehead. Behind him a small golden ring with strange carved markings appears spinning slowly the ring levitates on its own. Scrat's eyes open shinning red in the darkness he smiles at Katz.

Ragnor speaks, "Well Katz it has been some time since we have seen each other face to face like this."

Katz stares in annoyance hearing the voice of Ragnor coming from Scrat's mouth he responds. "Let me guess dragon you were simply using him and now you have completely possessed him like you did to me once?"

Ragnor responds, "Yes exactly but it isn't like that matters now. You will remove your soul from that shell and I will take it."

Katz cocks an eyebrow up, "What…! No…that makes no sense."

Ragnor raises his hand, "Then you leave me no choice."

Katz rolls his eyes, "I wasn't going to give you an option anyway."

The two dart towards each other slamming their fist together they create a large shockwave from the impact. Katz falters back as Ragnor rushes in capitalizing with a hard right fist. The attack knocks Katz from the air sending him skating across the water. Katz flips over catching himself he slides onto the beach while looking upward at the possessed Scrat. "Let's see if I can end this quick."

Katz lifts both hands upward creating a triangle with his fingertips he captures Ragnor in the center of the triangle. A ball of atomic energy builds up filling the space between his hands. The energy pulsates while Ragnor looks down seeing the light he juts out one of his own arms his palm is outlined with a red light as he unleashes a red beam towards his foe. Katz counters with his own blast. The two streams clash high over the water flashing constantly as they push against each other.

Katz begins to slide back along the sand as his stream of energy weakens slowly being engulfed by the attack from Ragnor. The dragon grins pushing more of his power into the attack he drives back Katz's blast to the edge of his fingers, "Crap he does have a lot of power. This won't be as easy as I thought."

Katz jumps from the ground as the blast slams into the shore exploding in a large ball of fire. Katz flies high barely avoiding the explosion as he floats above the towering flames Ragnor teleports in front of him striking Katz with a hard punch to the gut. He coughs while Ragnor spins quickly bringing down his leg in an attempt to smash Katz's neck. He grabs the boot swinging Ragnor around before tossing him across the sky before firing off an atomic blast.

The dragon is thrown back by the explosion regaining his balance he looks around only to get punched in the head by Katz. Ragnor drops down holding his head in pain he turns upwards opening his mouth he releases a torrent of dragon fire igniting the sky above. Katz drops out of the air splashing down into the lake as his cape burns down to nothing. He floats around extinguishing the flames before dashing back up to the surface.

As he peeks through the surface of the water Ragnor grabs him by the head holding Katz up he punches him square in the face. Katz rockets over the water surface and into a beach house bleeding heavily from his nose and forehead he crawls up to his feet. He looks outside seeing Ragnor jetting over the water towards him. Katz then opens a small dimensional portal above the palm of his hand from the tear a long jagged sword appears. Grabbing the blade by the hilt he flies out of the beach house catching Ragnor by surprise as he impales him with the blade driving it through his chest.

"Gotcha," Katz whispers to Ragnor before taking the hilt with both hands and twisting the sword cutting through Ragnor's innards.

Katz takes one hand setting it directly in front of Ragnor's eyes he fires a full blast of atomic energy burning away at Ragnor's face. Ragnor yells before teleporting away back into the city. The dragon falls over holding his burned and scarred face in pain while blood pours out of his open wound.

He attempts to regenerate but nothing happens. "Damn…that man, little man….and this worthless body. I can't generate enough power to subdue him. Well I'll just have to kill him."

Katz arrives at the shore falling to his knees he breathes heavily, "Ugh…that is draining. He better be done. I'm practically out of energy." From above the other characters appear flying down to him landing along the beach each bruised and wounded.

Monos walks over to Katz helping him to his feet. "Katz what happened and how can we help?"

Katz looks out at Chicago on fire and in ruins, "He's still out there. Scrat lost control and the dragon is back in his own slick body at that. I stabbed him with this sword, and shot him in the face with as much power as I could muster at that moment, but then he vanished. I'm sure he isn't dead…but really I can't keep this up. Although I am hoping that he just quits now…."

"Boss!" Arcos shuffles over to Katz carrying Titallic on his shoulder, "Boss you got to help, I don't think he is going to make it."

Katz looks up to Arcos then over to Titallic staring at the gaping hole in his abdomen he grabs Titallic from Arcos laying him down on the sand. "Just give me a second." Holding one hand over the wound his hand glows shinning a light over Titallic's gut. Trillions of atoms sew themselves together restoring Titallic's body slowly as the light passes over his wound. Katz lifts his hand standing up again he wipes the sand from his clothes. "Done."

Titallic sits up feeling better he looks down at torso seeing nothing but his abdominals he looks up seeing the others and Katz around him.

"Boss your back and you healed me!" Titallic says as he pulls himself up from the sand.

Katz rolls his eyes, "Don't let it go to your head. There will be time for discussion and pleasantries later, you know how much energy you just cost me…all of it. I'm spent and the dragon is still alive. Prepare the defenses!"

A plume of dirt and smoke rises from the city as Ragnor dashes out from behind the buildings he rushes out onto the beach. The characters take up defensive stances as Ragnor slides over the sand swaying in and out around each of the characters.

He tackles Katz taking him over the water the two dart upwards high into the atmosphere. Ragnor smirks, "Now you die."

Katz struggles to break free drained of energy he fails miserably as the dragon lifts him into space. Katz struggles gasping for air unable to gather any oxygen his body slowly begins to freeze over. "What's the matter…a little cold for you? I guess you haven't learned how to survive out here yet…too bad."

Ragnor releases Katz flying over him he stomps on him. The two fall towards the earth building up heat around them. They fall like a meteor towards the Earth as Katz's arm shatters under the pressure melting away in the atmosphere while Ragnor drills his hand into Katz's chest. Ragnor then gives Katz a farewell nod before releasing a burst of energy through Katz's body.

A large explosion covers the sky above the city streaming across the darkness as the others look up in shock. Ragnor descends to the beach landing ahead of the characters while burnt remains fall from the sky.

Arcos and the others stand frozen in shock and fear while the dragon dusts his armor off, "That damn fool made quite a hole in my armor and he ruined my face but I took care of him. Now for the rest of you!"

Sparks crackle in the eyes of Albert and Sentry as the two blitz towards Ragnor throwing a barrage of rapid punches and kicks at the dragon. Ragnor evades a few blows, but he finds himself out matched as the two begin to bludgeon him pummeling him into the ground. The dragon vanishes teleporting away he appears behind Arcos and Titallic.

"What's up boys?" Ragnor says with a smile.

Titallic turns delivering a hard metal punch to Ragnor's face knocking him back into a wall. As he falters forward Arcos rushes in striking him with multiple kicks. Ragnor grabs his leg stopping the attack he blasts Arcos back with a beam from his mouth. Arcos rolls back bleeding from the attack he falls flat face down. Titallic discharges hundreds of volts of electricity striking the wall as Ragnor runs dodging the blast. The dragon dashes up to Titallic placing both hands on his metal chest releases an explosive blast. Titallic flies back smashing into a building he loses his metal form as he falls on the road below. Ragnor then teleports over to Ralph grabbing his arm he pulls hard tearing it from its socket he kicks the bleeding warrior away. Ragnor throws the hand on the ground.

Landlord molds the earth around the dragon trying to trap him. He claps his hands together in an attempt to crush the dragon, but the flames melt the rock and earth. Brainstorm and Albert rain down horrific lightning on Ragnor as the electricity strikes him he staggers falling down to one knee. More blood drips out of his chest wound while half of his face melts revealing his bones.

His body sizzles with electric energy as Ragnor turns his sights on the rest of the characters flashing over the ground he unloads millions of black tendrils rip through their bodies and into the ground. Hawkins pulls himself up with his tentacles standing on his feet he rips the tendrils from his body.

"We aren't done yet!" Hawkins yells as he claps his hands together creating a heavy shockwave.

The waves roll over the shore, knocking Ragnor with heavy winds, forcing him back he loses control of his tendril attack. As he looks out Hawkins appears in front of him smashing his fist into Ragnor's side he causes the dragon to fall down nearly crippled. Hawkins then drives an uppercut at the dragon, but he grabs Hawkins's hand reversing his strength he lifts Hawkins up dropping him head first into the ground.

Ragnor coughs up blood breathing heavily he takes off flying high into the air. "That's it! I'm done with this!"

He lifts his right hand out into the sky. Sparks fly from his fingertips as energy begins to swirl around morphing itself into an orb. The orb expands into a large sphere covering a section of the sky the red and black energy flashes constantly.

"Well it has been fun, there hasn't been anyone to push me this far in many millennia but now....it is time to remove all of you. I'll just take all the energy left in that useless man's soul to purge you from my planet." Ragnor says as his eyes are filled with darkness.

"Well dudes...ugh...I'm missing an arm and that looks really strong." Ralph says as he staggers across the beach holding his stump.

Tyreal shakes his head, "Monos we can't stop that...we don't have the energy for this."

Monos floats in the air bleeding from the entry wounds from the tendrils, "Brainstorm do you have a plan? I can probably fly up there and hold it off for a while."

Brainstorm nods breathing heavily, "I can...ugh put up one last field around it to try and contain it at best but even then...it will keep going after I'm done. That attack is strong enough to destroy the planet. We need more help."

Monos falls in terror, "Darn...it just can't end like this. We have to come up with something."

Landlord responds to Monos, "Can't we force it to explode above us? Or maybe I can build a wall of earth to protect us."

Monos speaks, "It isn't just us that we have to worry about you heard Brainstorm. That attack is too powerful."

Titallic steps forward, "Brainstorm you just have to contain it for a short while. I'll make sure that it never hits."

"What are you going to do?" asks Brainstorm.

"Just get the barrier ready." Titallic expends the last of his energy mutating into his metal form he takes off flying quickly up to Ragnor.

The dragon, seeing Titallic flying towards him, tosses the gargantuan sphere down at the surface of the planet. Titallic runs into the sphere placing both hands on it he tries to force the energy back while building up all the electricity remaining in his body. Brainstorm's eyes turn purple as he begins to wrap the sphere in a psychic barrier.

Ragnor squints with his one remaining eye, seeing the psychic barrier he holds out his other hand firing a single beam of energy. The beam runs through the sphere piercing Titallic's chest it forces him out of the sky. As the beam continues forward it shifts sliding along the ground it strikes Brainstorm knocking him over before exploding on the shore. The sphere continues to speed towards the ground as the characters look on in horror.

Chapter 19: Beginnings

Cosmic flames erupt in the sky as a pillar of flame descends towards the ground. Large wings of fire swirl around the characters brushing away the sphere of energy and sending it far into space. The flames then burst forth from the ground encircling Ragnor as he looks around confused. Rage builds across his face as a shape forms before him. Red and gold boots appear standing on a disc of fire golden armor adorns the man's body along with golden red gauntlets on his hands. Ragnor looks up seeing the flames pull back to reveal Dr. Katz with a smirk on his face and fire burning from his eyes. Jets of fire recede from his back as the fire in his eyes slowly dies.

"Damn it! You weren't fully combined with the phoenix beforehand when I killed you! How is this possible!?"

Katz crosses his arms, "Ragnor...you know so little. The bird and I came to an agreement long before I beat you up. It would seem that bird is still being useful in reviving me after my untimely demise at your hands no less."

Ragnor hisses, "Grrr....little man...you never cease to amaze me. This is why you will be my vessel. Now come you see this body is falling apart."

Katz sighs, "That it is, could be because you burned too much energy, could also be because you were beaten. Now it's time to end this."

Ragnor grins at Katz waving his hand at him, "Come Katz to the end!"

Jets of flame ignite from Katz's back as he dashes through the air heading directly for Ragnor. The dragon engulfs his body in black flames turning into a fireball he rushes back driving towards his foe. Katz concentrates a mass of fire into his right hand; striking back against the black fireball as the energy from the attacks ripples down to the surface tearing apart the ground and creating waves on the lake. Katz's eyes ignite with flames as he pushes harder shattering the fireball he smashes his fist across Ragnor's face.

The dragon rolls through the sky stunned by the attack he gasps for air feeling his power slipping. Katz spreads his hands out engulfing his body in flame he dashes towards Ragnor transforming into a blazing phoenix he rushes through the dragon skating along the air behind him. Ragnor's entire body bursts into flames, illuminating the sky.

Katz turns around watching the embers blow around him and Ragnor he stares into the dragon's eye. "It's finished," he says.

The dragon shrugs, "Oh Katz...hahahaha. How little you know little man. Nothing is ever truly finished. I'll be sure to make you remember that."

Katz cocks one eyebrow up, "You are obviously delusional. I hear people get like that when they see death before them. Anyway your times up."

Ragnor stare at Katz closing his eye he smirks, "You just don't know what you have done little man. I am eternal....I cannot be destroyed so easily. You think you have won, but you will seek me when the time is right. And I will be there ready to take my vessel. Until next time...K.S. Katz. Ha-ha...."

Scrat's body explodes in a large black fire a whirlwind of energy dissipates as rain begins to fall over the city. Katz lands on the beach looking over the group of characters as they stare in awe. The flames vanish from his back as he waves his hand over the group they are each set on fire. The flames dance over their bodies regenerating their missing limbs and healing their wounds before dissipating into the air.

The phoenix armor bursts into a puff of fire as Katz returns to normal he walks pass the group, hopping up on a wall he sits down breathing a sigh of relief. "Finally...now I can take a break."

He closes his eyes for a second when he is tackled from the wall falling on the ground he stares around seeing his team lifting him into the air with a cheer.

"Boss you're alive!!!" Sentry yells as they continue to cheer.

"Ugh ahh...what! It's good to see you all are full of energy! Now put me down!" They drop Katz as he staggers around slightly dizzy.

Titallic speaks, "Boss aren't you glad to be alive? We are glad to see you, we were worried!"

Katz nods, "Of course I can assure you being dead is no fun...and it hurts a lot. I suggest you all try not to do it if you can. I did see how you all fought and I must say I'm quite proud of all of you. You have done an amazing job and you have become much stronger than before."

Albert vaults over the wall while the others stroll around it meeting up with Katz and the villains. "Katz I'm glad you are still alive, but how did you do that?"

Hawkins chimes in, "The phoenix that he absorbed was able to restore his life though at what cost who knows."

Katz laughs, "Just at the cost of not being able to use that technique again for a couple of months I think. So if you want to kill me now is the opportune time, but once again that isn't fun and I would greatly advise you all not to do it."

Brainstorm rubs his chin looking out at the destroyed areas of the city his jaw drops. "Our home…the penthouse…it was in that area where we were battling. I think I remember seeing the building collapse…we have no home."

A deep feeling of regret flows over the heroes while Katz yawns. He turns his attention to Ralph. "Ralph I require a favor from you. It involves obtaining a building not right now obviously since you are tired and weakened but after you have recovered. So by tomorrow aye?"

Ralph squints, "What makes you think I'll do you any favors dude? I work for money or for revenge from losing my money."

Katz growls slowly, "Tomorrow."

"Well you know on second thought you did restore my arm and I haven't had as much fun in my life since I started working with you guys so I'm in yeah…haha." Ralph says with a change of tune.

Katz nods, "Good though you didn't need the act in the first place."

Monos strolls over to Katz, "What are you planning? Do you think we will have to fight again?"

Katz shrugs, "We are going to get our home back. As far as battling again I don't know, as far as fighting you guys again that is up to you. Either way I figured you all would need an invite to our new pad. It is only right after all, you guys took us in when we had no place to go. Aside from that you may want to talk to your team and see how it goes over. I can't imagine them saying no but still. I will converse with my group and see for myself. We could use the help building up the new place and it wouldn't be bad having some company there, I suppose."

Monos says, "Alright Katz I'll go speak to them. The heroes huddle around in a circle while Katz and the villains do the same. Arcos peeks up to see if he can hear what the heroes are saying when Katz grabs him pulling him back in. "Now boys what do you all think about those super humans over there?" Pointing towards Monos and his group Katz smirks.

"Well to be honest with you they aren't as bad as I first thought," Titallic says, "In fact working with Tyreal and Landlord was kind of fun actually."

Arcos scoffs, "They are weak…very weak. Yet still I do have a bit of respect for them, they did help us out more than once so they are fine with me."

"And you Sentry?" Katz asks.

Sentry thinks for a moment, "I don't mind them as much as I use to. After being stuck with them and actually talking with them. I can see them not getting in our way again. Also Tyreal has a pretty sweet gaming system…just so you know boss we took it from the house with all his games before the battle. It's safe and we can use it once we get the base up and running."

Katz's eyes ignite with energy, "Gaming, boy has it been some time since I did that. This is going to be awesome. Shall I go give them the news?"

Albert laughs, "We all will Katz." The two groups meet extending their hands they each shake in agreement.

"Hey Tyreal!!" Sentry yells, "We still have your game station and we will return it once the new base is complete. You'll be amazed at the stash that we have."

As the others continue their conversation Katz walks off jumping over a barrier he lands on the road. Before him he finds Wizencut spying from the side of the road. Wizencut attempts to take off running when Katz appears before him.

Wizencut bumps into him falling back on his bottom he looks up with terror. "Oh come now old man, if I wanted you dead you would already be dead. Anyway do attempt to inform your higher ups that we didn't kill you and that we basically saved all of your worthless souls from complete destruction by that dragon. Cross me again, and I can assure you it won't be so pleasant for you and your kin. Just because we are turning over a somewhat new leaf, does not mean I won't cross back into killing you guys without a second thought."

Katz then walks off leaving Wizencut there on the ground. He walks over finding Monos, Albert and Hawkins standing watching the others run around. "Well Katz fancy new group you have here to lead," Hawkins says.

Katz yawns, "Haha a group for me aye, well that isn't completely true but it works I guess. Monos I haven't forgotten what you and Brainstorm did that while ago, but I will work towards mending such relationships I suppose, you guys can't be that bad I guess. Or well, I mean, it looks like you are trying to be better so I might as well get over it."

Monos nods, "Thanks Katz, I'll do what I can as well. We are trying."

The steady rain begins to slow as light rises in the horizon. The dawn of a new day begins to creep over the lake.

Albert stretches looking up at the rising sun, "Dawn's approaching Katz, I have to go check in with Emily, but I'll be back to help with the building. We are getting married later this year; I'll get you all invitations."

Katz nods in approval, "Oh what an interesting time we will have this year. We are moving on to new beginnings it would seem. A bold new world it is! The four characters look over the shore while a gale of wind rushes over the calm lake water. Behind them the fires burn throughout the city as a building falls to the ground crumbling under the flames. Katz smiles, "Beginnings indeed now onward to tomorrow!"